EYELET WITNESS

JULIE ANNE LINDSEY

Cozy Queen
PUBLISHING

Dedicated to my Cozy Queens

A NOTE FROM THE AUTHOR

Hello Lovely Reader,

Thank you so much for joining me on Bonnie & Clyde's newest adventure! I hope you're having as much fun in Bliss as I am.

As you know, there will be eight novels in the Bonnie & Clyde Mysteries, along with additional, spin-off series, as secondary characters rise to the front and insist their stories be told. So, if you have a favorite, be sure to let me know!

You can keep in touch between the books via my Cozy Club newsletter.

And if you enjoy EYELET WITNESS, don't forget to grab your copy of FLARED STIFF.

Now, let's go check in with your favorite furry little outlaw!
  -Julie Anne Lindsey

I wet my lips as I reached for the Good Luck Falls calendar hanging on my office wall. My heart rate increased as I turned the page from January to February, putting last month and the images of local firemen behind me, eagerly anticipating what lie ahead.

As a kid growing up in rural Bliss, Georgia, I'd never understood the quiet whispers and general excitement that accompanied each new calendar. My mama, and what seemed like all the women in town, practically climbed over one another to get their hands on the new issue each year.

Fast forward a few decades, and I wholly understood the hype.

The annual Good Luck Falls calendar featured respected men from the community enjoying their jobs, the beloved waterfall, or other local recreation locations to their fullest. And the entire inventory always sold out in hours.

I hooked the new page in place and gave the man in blue jeans and a wet white t-shirt a long appraising look. He was playing fetch with his dog at the lake, and had apparently been splashed just enough so the soft cotton adhered to his very nice chest. He ran one hand through thick black hair, smiling at the racing pooch. The pose did nice things for his toned biceps and flat abdomen. Nothing obscene or even suggestive. Still, it was hard not to stare. Sunlight filtered through puffy white clouds illuminating his tan skin and accentuating the playful glint in his eyes. Basically, the photographer was a genius.

"Hello, Charles Miller," I said with a wink at the shiny page.

Charles Miller ran the local Lube Stop, and I suspected the line at his garage was about to double as women realized how badly they needed an oil change.

Creating and selling the Good Luck Falls calendars had begun as a charity effort that earned untold sums over the years, and all the money went to charity. For local ladies, and probably more than a few men, they were the gifts that kept on giving.

"Bonnie?" my teenage shopkeep, Lexi, called from the hallway outside my open office door. "Louisa's here!"

"Coming," I returned, pulling my eyes from the page. My boyfriend, the local sheriff, was featured somewhere in the calendar, but I wasn't sure where. So far I'd been able to stop myself from peeking, but it was only February. "See you later, Charles Miller," I told the calendar with a pat on my way out.

A few quick steps later, the short hallway spilled into the main sales floor of Bless Her Heart, my second-chance shop on the town square.

Lexi stood outside the circular checkout counter at the center of the space, chatting animatedly with our special guest, her former babysitter. Lexi's long dark hair hung down her back in poker-straight strands. Her wide brown eyes danced as she spoke to her friend.

Lexi had graduated from high school last summer and

been working with me ever since. She hadn't decided on a career direction beyond shopkeep, and I wasn't in a hurry to complain. She was talented and helpful. Courteous and kind. Much as I hoped she'd find her passion and pursue it one day, I was glad to make the most of my time with her while she was here. And hopefully be an encouragement to her in the process.

"Louisa," I said, hurrying to greet the twenty-something blonde with a hug. "I'm so glad you called."

Louisa was Lexi's former babysitter, and from what I could tell, no more than five or six years her senior.

To my thirty-nine-year-old eyes, they both looked like babies, but I didn't envy their youth. I'd made far too many mistakes in mine. Honestly, for a woman pushing forty, I was possibly the happiest I'd ever been.

"Thank you for offering your help," Louisa said. "I just about squealed when Lexi said you had some things for me to take a look at." She set her pink pet carrier onto the counter, and the distinctly disgruntled cluck of a chicken followed. "Hush now, Thelma," she whispered. "Not every-thing can be about you."

My sleek black cat, Clyde, poked his head out from beneath a chair in my window display, intrigued by the sound of a feathered friend. The small silver bell on his crimson bowtie jingled softly in response to the move.

Clyde and I coordinated our ensembles whenever possi-ble, and this month, we were wearing red for the holiday. His bowtie was a near-perfect color match for my vintage struc-tured dress and pumps.

Louisa unfastened the single silver button of her long, navy cape and frowned. "I guess this actually *is* about you, though, isn't it?" she asked the bird.

I took her coat while Clyde slinked in the counter's direction. I flashed him a warning look, and he stilled, as if I might not see him if he didn't move.

Louisa smoothed a hand over the skirt of her ankle-length green and navy plaid dress. Her long golden hair was rolled into loose barrel curls and pinned up on both sides. She'd dashed her long dark lashes in mascara and added a sheen of gloss over her lips. The biting February wind had added natural color to her cheeks. She looked more like a porcelain doll from another era than a human in search of the perfect dress for a chicken judging.

My red hair, fair skin and hazel eyes probably made me look like Raggedy Ann.

"Let me show you what I've got," I said, leading her to a pair of old dresses I'd revitalized with her in mind. "I adjusted the hems and updated the necklines, but I thought the colors and patterns were just your style."

"Oh," she cooed, excitedly following me toward the clothing racks. "Thank you so much for doing this. I never know what to wear to the poultry evaluations. It always seems so important that I look just right, even though the judges are supposed to be focused on Thelma."

Thelma and Louisa were all-stars in the local chicken circuit. Thelma being a blue ribbon-winning hen, many times over, and Louisa being a popular breeder on the rise.

"It's no problem," I assured her. "Making old things new again is what I do."

In a farming community, where every penny counted, I'd learned to spruce up and reinvent castoff items very early on. Seeing the beauty and possibility in everything was probably a side effect of being raised on a flower farm. In some ways, Bless Her Heart was the lovechild of those qualities and skills. The shop had also been my salvation after I'd moved home and opened the doors amidst a messy divorce last year.

Now, I helped everyone I could, however I could. And

that included lovely young hen breeders and their puffy Polish chickens.

Lexi followed us to a seating arrangement outside my curtained dressing rooms. The pair of armchairs were taupe, cream and tan. The rug was braided crimson and pink to match the overstuffed throw pillows I'd propped on each cushion. She placed Thelma's crate on the little rug and took a seat on the floor beside it.

"What do you think?" I asked, motioning to the pair of dresses in question.

Louisa held the dresses against her, one, then the other, peering down at them with unbridled pleasure. "I love these," she said. "Both of them. Goodness. How do I choose?"

Lexi laughed. "Maybe try them on?"

"Right." Louisa smiled, then hurried into a changing room and pulled the curtain.

"You can have them both, if you like them on," I said. "You don't have to choose."

Louisa squeaked with glee. "All the other breeders wear pantsuits, but I'm just not comfortable in those. I don't even own any dress pants. I can't understand what's wrong with being a lady in a dress," she said. "Why can't I be feminine and a good farmer?"

"You can," I said, thinking instantly of my mama, who was inarguably feminine but also one heck of a flower farmer. Mama loved her overalls, and I couldn't imagine her in anything else for a long day of work. But Louisa loved her old-fashioned dresses and petit fours, whatever the occasion. Who was to say one was right and the other wrong?

Louisa lived what she called a "cottagecore lifestyle." Apparently cottagecore was a movement that focused on simple living, self-sufficiency and harmony with nature. She lived in a community dedicated to her way of life, located in the rival town next door.

"Ooo," Louisa cooed behind the curtain. "This is so cute. I think I like this one even more on."

I stood a little taller with her compliment, and at five-two, good posture made a difference.

Lexi smiled. "Come out. Let's see," she said, stroking Thelma's feathered head through the carrier's door.

Louisa emerged in a violet smock dress that hit mid-calf. The casual garment had a loose fit, coming in only a smidge at the ribs, above her waistline. I'd added a delicate eyelet trim at the hem and cuffs.

She spun and the material rose in a puff. "I love it," she said.

"Cute," Lexi agreed. "What will the judges think?"

Louisa chewed her lip. "I don't know. I'm the youngest breeder, and it's hard to be taken seriously no matter what I do. Even if my hens are far superior." She sighed. "It's also possible I'm overthinking. Ben got in my head, and it's been hard to shake him."

I looked to Lexi as Louisa returned to her dressing room. "Who's Ben?"

"Her ex-boyfriend," Lexi said. "He was obsessed with trying to monetize her and Thelma."

I wrinkled my nose. "Monetize them?"

"He wasn't from my community," Louisa called over the curtain. "He couldn't let go of his obsession with money. The breakup was ruthless, but it's over now. That's what counts. Thelma and I are doing just fine without him and his constant negativity."

She peeled back the curtain and stepped into view once more, this time striking a pose in an ice-blue wool dress. "All his business talk probably contributed to my pursuit of the soufflé stand," she said. "So, I can't complain about that. Once my stand is up and running, all those eggs my hens give me can be used to make quiches and soufflés. Then that money can go back into raising the hens. It's brilliant, actually. Chicken breeding isn't cheap."

"Sounds like a perfect cycle to me."

She beamed.

Lexi frowned. "Is Ben still bothering you about Thelma?"

"Not really," she said, as I asked, "Bothering you how?"

Louisa gave a dramatic sigh. "He was sure she'd win a big advertising contract if I pushed her into modeling and acting."

I eyeballed the little pink carrier, wondering how well any hen could model or act.

"He thought I was wasting her talent," Louisa went on. "He tried to take her in the split."

"Good grief," I said, heartsick at the thought of anyone attempting to take Clyde from me.

"But he lost, of course," Louisa said, grinning. "Thelma is all mine. Take them apples, Ben Reid."

Louisa turned to the full-length mirror and gave her reflection a long look. "I'm just glad it's over. We like the simple life. Right, Thelma?"

The chicken cocked its head and released a sharp *bawk-ah!*

Clyde jumped straight up, having crept stealthily along the carrier until the hen went off. His fur flared and his tail puffed, as if he'd been electrocuted. When his paws hit the ground, he was already running.

Thelma craned her neck, clucking low and steadily, either warning my cat or laughing at him.

The low hum of power tools drew Louisa's attention to a set of etched glass doors on one interior wall. She frowned a moment before meeting my eyes. "I'm going to miss the coffee shop," she said, referring to the best place to get a caffeine fix in all of Bliss. Until recently, it had been on the other side of those doors. "But I think it's wonderful the new owner will be serving Blissful Bean's coffee in their bakery."

I smiled. "The new owner is my grandmama Gigi. She adores Dave and his coffee. She wouldn't have it any other way."

The glass doors were covered in paper from the bakery's side, but I'd been taking sneak peeks at the construction work for months. There'd been more to do than I realized. Transforming a basic, last-century coffee shop with a massive counter and limited seating into Gigi's idea of a perfect confectionary escape was not without its challenges.

Oh, My Goodies had been a lifetime in the making for Gigi, and much of Bliss held its collective breath in anticipation of opening day. Me included.

"Miss Eggers?" A man in a puffed black coat and knit cap entered the front door, bringing with him a gust of icy wind.

We jumped in response.

"Oh! Good morning," I called. "Welcome to Bless Her Heart."

I moved in his direction when he remained steadfast on the mat inside my door. "I didn't hear the bells over the noise," I explained, tipping my head in the direction of Oh, My Goodies. "How can I help you?"

"I'm looking for Ms. Louisa Eggers," he repeated, returning my smile only slightly.

Louisa tiptoed in our direction on socked feet. "I'm Louisa Eggers."

The man passed her a large manila envelope. "You've been served," he said, then spun and walked away, leaving us in another burst of frigid air.

"What on earth?" Louisa whispered, quickly opening the envelope and unearthing its contents. A flush rose over her skin as she read, turning her cheeks scarlet and shaping her mouth into a little o. "Ben is suing me for custody of Thelma!"

CHAPTER TWO

*L*ouisa flopped into an armchair, wadded tissues pressed to her puffy eyes.

I uncapped a bottle of water from the mini fridge I kept beside my refreshments table and passed it to her. "Here. Drink."

She accepted the offering with a whimper, then a soft growl. "I hate that he can get me upset like this without even showing up," she said, pressing the bottle to her lips. She drank greedily, brows furrowed. "I'm a nice person, and I always try to do the right thing. How did I ever date someone like him?" she asked, clearly baffled. "How can he think he's entitled to shared custody of my hen? Just because he helped care for her while we were together?"

I groaned, and she turned the thin stack of papers in my direction.

"He's claiming to have contributed financially to Thelma's well-being, and apparently thinks that qualifies as a vested interest." She set her bottle aside with shaking fingers. "He bought feed for all the hens once, because he said he wanted to."

I scanned the offered papers, still clutched in her white-knuckled fingers. "What's this line about enrichment materials and housing?" I asked, squinting to read the single-space print.

Louisa made a disgusted, throaty noise. "I put money aside for months to purchase a new hen house. I even cancelled my chicken cam service to help save faster, but when it was time to buy, Ben went with me and ruined it."

I patted her shoulder, understanding the loss.

When I'd first met Louisa, she'd shown me live footage of her hens, using a camera on their end, and a phone app on hers. The concept seemed a little excessive, but adorable, and I knew I'd cheerfully spy on Clyde if I could.

"When we got there," she continued, "Ben insisted I upgrade, and he immediately started talking to the carpenter about all the available options. When I told them both I was on a firm budget, Ben said he wanted to pitch in because I'd been looking forward to it for so long. He called his contribution a gift. I was so flabbergasted and uncomfortable, I went along with it." She dropped her hand into her lap, pulling the papers away.

I frowned. "I'm sorry."

Lexi sat at her feet, Thelma's crate by her side. "Men are dumb," Lexi said.

"And mean," Louisa said.

I sighed and lowered into the chair beside hers. "I'm sorry this is happening. Do you need help finding an attorney?" I paused, considering my offer. How did someone go about locating an attorney effectively versed in chicken custody battles? Was that even a thing?

"No," she said. "Not yet. Ben has money that I don't. He could bankrupt me if I fight him on this legally, and that would mean giving up my soufflé stand. I'm not ready to do that."

"Bawk-ah!" Thelma complained, causing me to jump once more.

"Don't worry," Louisa told her pet. "I'm going to try to talk to him. Maybe he'll see sense and withdraw this stupid lawsuit."

I felt her agony in my bones, having just completed a messy court battle with my ex. "We'll figure this out," I promised. "You won't lose your soufflé stand if I can help it."

Louisa turned misty blue eyes to me. "I hope you're right."

"I am."

She forced a small smile. "Any chance you want to help me decorate it on a teeny tiny budget? Because Ben has never been one to actually see reason. He usually only sees dollar signs," she said, her natural southern drawl tugging on every word.

I smiled back. "Absolutely."

Lexi pulled her knees to her chest and wrapped her arms around them. "I'm excellent at creating million-dollar looks for pocket change. Maybe I can help."

"Sold," Louisa said. "That will probably be all I have left when this is over."

I nudged her gently. "That and two incredible dresses."

Louisa laughed. "They are pretty great dresses."

"And you have friends," Lexi said. "Real ones, and a great community that cares about you and Thelma. This will be okay. Ben has no idea who he's messing with."

I hoped she was right. I wanted her to be right. But I knew money talked, and when a spiteful opportunist had the money, things could get difficult for the good guys. "Ben knows he can't gain any kind of custody or ownership based on a few contributions to her feed and toys," I told her. "He's just trying to scare and manipulate you. No sane judge would remove a pet from a loving home and give it to a man who came in and out of your life."

She nodded, straightening in her seat. "He always does this. I don't know why I let him. He has some weird way of confusing me all the time, and I'm not a dumb person. Or I didn't used to be."

Lexi scoffed. "You are not dumb. He's awful. He uses people. You're kind, and he took advantage. Dumping him already proved you're smarter than him."

Louisa laughed.

Lexi cast me a curious look, then pointed to the pink crate. "Can Thelma come out for a minute?" She dragged her gaze to Louisa then. "She's been in here a long time."

Louisa shrugged. "She doesn't mind, and I'm on my way out anyhow. I found two perfect dresses."

"It's no bother," I said, stretching onto my feet. "Give me just a sec to find my little Houdini so he doesn't give her a scare."

Thelma clucked as I hunted for Clyde and Lexi coaxed her from her carrier.

"What made you break up with Ben?" Lexi asked Louisa. "Was there a final straw?"

"Not really. We weren't compatible as humans, for starters. He was too interested in how I could make more money, and didn't want to hear I was already happy. He was obsessed with taking Thelma to Hollywood, and he was jealous of other men. He thought I flirted with the local lumberjack and blacksmith."

I frowned at the lengthy list of reasons for telling Ben to kick stone.

"Who are the lumberjack and blacksmith?" Lexi asked, eager to hear more about the alleged other men.

I spotted Clyde on a shelf behind my counter and swept him into my arms for a snuggle.

"They're the same person," Louisa said. "Eli Fogle." Her voice was dreamy, and I wanted to hear the rest.

Clyde pushed out of my arms as I dallied, hoping to hear the rest of Louisa's story.

He darted under a rack of dresses, and I followed back in the ladies' direction.

"He doesn't know I'm alive," she said. "He's older than me, and he's a little brooding sometimes. He keeps to himself more than the rest of us, but he's always patient and considerate. I think someone hurt him once," she said, sounding as if the possibility hurt her too. "That's why he came to our community, but he doesn't talk about it. A cheating spouse maybe."

"Spouse?" Lexi said. "You think he was married?"

Louisa shrugged. "Maybe. He's gorgeous and kind to the core. He's probably thirty, and I can't imagine he's never been in love."

"Have you?" Lexi asked. "Ever been in love?"

Louisa's small pink mouth pulled into a frown once more. "No."

Lexi fell back onto the rug, arms splayed and eyes pointed at the row of refinished chandeliers I'd mounted overhead. "I want to fall in love."

I bit my tongue. Too old and jaded to partake in their carefree discussion.

My therapist thought I should try to unpack my negative feelings on love and relationships so I could heal from past traumas and embrace new possibilities. I was working on it, but somedays love felt a lot like quicksand.

Thelma flapped her wings, and Clyde appeared before her. She craned her neck, examining him with one beady black eye, while I sneaked up behind him, praying he wouldn't attack her.

"Bawk-ah!"

Clyde collapsed. He stretched a paw in her direction, then rolled onto his back.

"I'm a sucker for a man who takes control," Louisa said. "Leaders are my catnip. Oh, look, I think they're making friends!"

I smiled, cautiously. Clyde had delivered more than one lifeless rodent and sparrow to my doorstep, pleased as a peacock for his hunting skills.

"Lawmen are my favorite," Louisa continued, "but Cromwell's police department is the worst. There are only three officers and one is a woman. No one really knows what they do other than drive around and nod. Eli is a little like Meadowbrook's law enforcement. He steps in to keep the peace when disagreements get out of hand. He can be tough, but he's always kind."

Meadowbrook was the name of the cottagecore community where Louisa lived in Cromwell. As far as I could tell, the group was mostly self-sufficient. They homeschooled their young, grew their own food and apparently policed their own people.

"Oh, and have you seen the sheriff?" She fanned her face.

Lexi looked in my direction, a mischievous smile growing. "You know the sheriff?"

"Not personally, per se," she said. "But have you seen him?" Louisa let her mouth fall open in exaggerated awe. "Someone, please fry an egg on him, because he is hot."

I snorted, unable to suppress a goofy grin and tiny laugh.

The bells over my shop's front door jingled, and Mason walked in, as if on cue.

He pulled a ballcap from his head, leaving his brown hair slightly tussled and exposing the flecks of gray at his brow and temples. His pale-blue eyes scanned the shop, and he smiled when he spotted us. "Ladies."

Louisa blushed furiously and Lexi smiled.

Thelma and Clyde were nowhere to be seen.

"Why do I feel as if I'm interrupting something?" he

asked, curiosity lifting one brow.

Lexi sat up. "You're not," she said. "We were just talking."

Louisa waved shyly.

I peeked under racks and around display stands as I went to greet Mason at the counter. "What brings you around, Sheriff?"

"You," he said, grinning mischievously, the only way he knew how. "I was in the area, so I thought I'd stop by."

"Lucky me," I said.

Mason had been checking on me regularly since we met last year. He'd relocated from Cleveland, Ohio after losing someone he cared about while undercover. I'd only been back in Bliss a few months at the time. We became good friends once he finished accusing me of murder, and just before Thanksgiving he'd confessed a romantic interest in me.

I'd agreed to pursue that matter, slowly, and we'd kissed under a star-filled sky. It was one of many similarly delightful encounters shortly thereafter, but he'd become progressively preoccupied since Christmas, and I didn't like that at all.

But I was trying to focus on the positive.

"Do you know Louisa?" I asked, motioning to our pink-cheeked guest.

"I believe I do," he said, fixing her with his gaze. "We've met at the farmers' market."

She nodded, and her barrel curls bobbed. "You complimented my eggs."

Lexi made a choking noise, and Thelma began to cluck.

Mason's eyes widened as he searched for the source of the sound. "Is that a—"

Thelma strutted into view, cocking her over-feathered head to stare up at the six-foot-three-inch man before her. *Bawk, bawk, bawk.*

Mason's mouth pressed into a thin line.

Clyde pranced along behind her, keeping his distance while somehow managing to act as if they were playing a game.

Louisa scooped the bird into a cuddle, kissed her head, then tucked her back into the carrier. "Sorry," she said. "I guess she probably shouldn't be roaming loose in a nice store like this."

I turned an amused smile to Mason. He had a deep and long-standing fear of chickens, after being attacked by one as a child. The fact he was currently a grown man and comparable giant did nothing to diminish his feelings on the subject.

He shook his head and cleared his throat. "I was just surprised. That's all. It's not every day I see a chicken going shopping."

Louisa laughed.

Mason sobered as he looked more carefully in her direction. "You okay? Something happen?" he asked, presumably noticing her puffy eyes and flushed cheeks, without realizing the two had separate causes, and he was the reason for the latter.

Lexi rose and jammed her hands against her hips. "Her ex-boyfriend is suing for custody of Thelma," she said. "A stranger brought the papers here to serve her. Can you believe that? One minute she was trying on dresses for the poultry judging, and the next minute, she's being sued."

"Is Thelma your daughter?" Mason asked, a sincere note of sympathy in his tone.

Louisa frowned. "What? No. I don't have children."

He turned his puzzled face to me.

I smiled. "Thelma's the chicken," I whispered.

Mason blinked, comically slowly, lips falling into a deep frown. "Thelma is the chicken," he repeated.

"I've had her since she was just a chick," Louisa said. "She imprinted on me when she was very young, and I've always been her main caregiver, so I suppose I am her mother. In some ways. Not that I want to take anything away from her biological mother, of course."

"Of course," he echoed, then turned fully to face me, pointing his back to the others. "I'm going to go now," he said softly. "Call me later?"

"Why were you at the Cromwell farmers' market?" Lexi asked, coming to stand beside us, Louisa's new dresses folded over one arm. "Isn't that a long way to go for produce?"

"Not at all," Louisa said. "He doesn't live but a few minutes away." She followed with Thelma in her crate.

"What do you mean?" Lexi asked, shifting her attention from her friend to Mason and back.

"Sheriff Wright lives on Cromwell Lake."

Lexi's jaw dropped.

I covered my mouth with curled fingers, hiding a laugh.

Historically, folks in Bliss didn't like the folks in Cromwell, our neighboring town. It was an ongoing rivalry, of which no one likely knew the origins. But we all did our part in keeping the animosity alive. With the occasional exception.

"Technically," Mason said. "I own a couple acres along the water. I plan to build a cabin one day, when I've got the time. Until then, the boat serves me well enough. I'd appreciate you not spreading any of that around," he said. "You know how people are about these towns. I don't want to drudge up unnecessary hostility—or anyone showing up unannounced."

Lexi closed her mouth, then mimed locking her lips with a key.

Tears rolled over Louisa's cheeks, and she pulled a fresh wad of tissues from the box on my counter. "Sorry." She waved the tissues helplessly. "I just can't believe I'm being sued. Or that I could lose Thelma, even part time. Or that Ben would stoop so low."

Mason's expression turned slightly sour. "Sounds to me like Ben's a bozo. Suing you for custody of your…"—he glanced at the carrier in her arms—"pet…is tasteless and desperate. I'm sure he'll move on when he realizes you aren't going to let her go without a fight."

Louisa seemed to consider this, and she straightened. "Right."

"Meanwhile, let me know if there's anything I can do to help," he said, then took another step toward the door.

I walked him out as Lexi moved around the counter to ring up Louisa's dresses. "Feeling okay?" I asked.

He looked behind me, to the closed door. "Mm hmm."

"That was nice of you to encourage her," I said. "She needed it, I think. Exes are the worst."

He dragged his eyes to me, and his expression softened. "How are things going with your ex? Anything new?"

I shook my head. Grant was dealing with the courts over his attempt to hide a whole lot of money from me, and the system, during our divorce. Thankfully, Mason's friend Dale, from the FBI Cyber Crimes division, was able to ferret it out. The courts divided our assets fairly, and I was doing much better. So was Gigi—I was bankrolling her new bakery. Grant, on the other hand, was being held accountable for his crime. "He calls," I said. "I don't answer."

"Any chance he wants to apologize?" Mason asked.

I rolled my eyes.

Grant had been calling incessantly since the first of the year. I'd been dodging him. I was working hard to put that part of my life behind me. Healing from the damage he'd done over the course of nineteen years wasn't easy, and I wasn't in any mood to muck up my progress.

"You can file harassment charges over these calls," Mason

said. "If they get to be too much, I can help. Your phone logs every time he tries to reach you. Have you kept the messages?"

"I don't think it's come to all that yet. He's mostly harmless. Manipulative and selfish, but otherwise a weasel."

"Weasels are predatory," Mason said. "Ask anyone with a hen house. If you change your mind, let me know."

I nodded. "I will."

"Until then, can I interest you in dinner at my place?"

"Maybe," I said, my mood immediately lifting. "Are you cooking?"

He smiled, and mischief returned to his eyes. "Does it count if I buy a quart of loaded baked potato soup and loaf of bread from the pub, then reheat them in my oven?"

"Sure."

"Then, yes," he said. "I'm cooking. Care to kiss the cook?"

I curled my fingers into the material of his jacket. "Goof."

Mason kissed me sweetly on the cheek, then straightened as my shop door opened and Louisa emerged. "I'll see you around seven," he said, striding off after a cautious look at Thelma's crate.

Louisa frowned. "I hope he didn't rush off on my account."

"Not at all," I said. "Did you get everything?"

"I think so," she said. "Thank you again for the beautiful dresses. I couldn't have made them for this price. It's wonderful. I hope you'll come by and see my soufflé stand when you have a chance. We can make some loose plans for the design, assuming I don't have to give my savings to a lawyer."

"I will," I said. "And you won't."

"I'd better not." She hiked her quilted bag higher on her shoulder. "Just to be sure, I'm going to see a bozo about a lawsuit."

CHAPTER THREE

he rest of the day dragged on, as many days had since winter arrived, driving everyone inside with its unwelcomed temperatures. Mason claimed it wasn't cold, but I'd never survive anywhere that -20 degrees and snow up to my knees were commonplace for a quarter of the year.

Thankfully, Lexi didn't mind keeping an eye on the shop while I visited Gigi to pass a few minutes before closing time.

I'd waited for the sounds of power tools and rumbling male voices to taper before considering a visit. I hadn't wanted to interfere or slow the progress while workers were still onsite, but the space beside mine had been still since six, so I went to knock on the etched glass doors between our shops.

A long shadow stretched over the paper covering the door, and the deadbolt rolled.

"Come in!" Gigi called, motioning me inside with a wicked grin. She set her broom against the wall and wiped her hands on her apron. Gigi was one of three nearly identical woman; my mama and I were the other two. Seeing us together had always been like looking at an age-progression photograph. Mama and Gigi had both become mothers as teens and produced a tiny replica of themselves for the effort. The red hair, fair skin and hazel eyes were passed down from our Irish lineage. As were our petite builds and big mouths. All things our ancestors would surely approve of.

"I wondered how long it would take you to pop in," she said, brushing dust from her long-sleeved t-shirt and jeans. "You made it thirty-five minutes since the last worker headed home."

"It wasn't easy to wait," I said, hugging her tight before scanning the former coffee shop. "I love seeing the day-to-day changes." I stepped around her to admire the bakery.

She'd removed the massive counter, which had previously occupied most of the dining area, and opened the space completely. Now, her service counter was just a small divider between the kitchen and front window, leaving plenty of room for tables, displays and décor.

"Most of the work happened in back today," she said. "The former stock room is officially a walk-in pantry and refrigerator, and the new cabinetry and ovens were installed. The glass display cases will go in by the register this week. All that's left to do then is fill the dining area with seating and ambience. I want a real fancy feel for my customers."

"I love all of that," I said, smiling back at Gigi.

Currently drywall dust coated everything in sight, and the shiny white floor was littered with debris, but I could still see her vision taking shape.

She went back to work with her broom while I made a slow circuit through the future bakery. "Tables and chairs are on order," she said. "I've got most of the décor picked out and stored in boxes until it's time to put the pieces together. Meanwhile, I want to apply white wainscoting and a chair rail, plus a lot of those wooden curlicue numbers near the ceiling."

I looked up to where she'd pointed. "Crown molding?"

"No, but that's coming," she said. "I chose the wide stuff. I mean those other doohickeys rich folks put in corners."

"Corbels?"

Gigi snapped her fingers. "That's them. I spoke to a local carpenter about adding built-in shelving along the wall near the window, and a padded window seat."

"Sounds beautiful," I said, in awe of the woman I never thought could impress me further.

Her shoulders relaxed. "I hope so."

"I know so. When's the big day?" She'd been hoping to open in January, but that month had officially ended at 12:01 this morning.

"I wanted to open on National Pie Day," she said. "That would've been perfect, but I missed it. Did you know almost every day is a national day of some kind? Later this month is National Do A Grump A Favor Day, and I'm going to tell Mirabelle her track suits are out of style."

I shook my head at her, fighting a smile. "Be nice."

Mirabelle was one of Gigi's lifelong friends. They had a unique on-again off-again relationship. Mirabelle was also the town's only crime reporter and desperately wanted to retire. Unfortunately, the local crime rate had increased a hundred fold since my return last year. So, it wasn't looking good for retirement.

Gigi shrugged. "I'm shooting for Valentine's Day now. That's always a good day for selling sweets. I'll run a special on chocolate-covered strawberries."

"Good thinking. You're going to be swamped. I'll help, if I can."

"I'd appreciate it," she said. "Your folks offered, but the

only thing busier than a bakery on Valentine's Day is a flower farm. They already hired extra help in preparation."

"I heard."

My phone rang, and I smiled.

"Sheriff Wright?" she guessed.

My smile fell when the screen came into view. "No. It's Grant."

Gigi made a soft gagging sound. "The only thing good that came from your time with that man is this bakery. Don't answer it."

I steeled my nerves and pressed the green button, choosing to take the opposite approach with Gigi at my side, rather than later, alone. Or worse, during dinner with Mason. He'd just keep calling back if I didn't take his call soon. Eventually I'd have to change my number.

She curled her lip in distaste.

"Hello, Grant," I said calmly, lifting a finger to tell Gigi I was making this quick. "I've asked you repeatedly to stop calling me, and I want you to know that if you call again, I will report you for harassment. I've spoken to local law enforcement about the matter, and I am well within my rights."

"Bonnie," he said, dragging my name out for several seconds. "I just need you to write an email to the judge on my behalf. Tell him I don't belong in jail. And I'll never call again. I promise," he said, his tone condescending as always. "After all I've done for you, you owe me this. Don't you think?"

I felt a familiar pull in my gut, the need to do as he asked, to keep the peace and get away before the situation escalated. Because when Grant didn't get his way, there was always a punishment.

Gigi dashed my shoes with her broom. "Whatever he's saying, tell him no," she whispered harshly. "No. No. No."

I sucked in a breath, having forgotten to breathe in the silent panic. "No," I said firmly, locking my eyes with Gigi.

She dipped her chin in silent affirmation, and a smile raised her wrinkled cheeks. She waved an enthusiastic thumb's up in my direction.

"What?" Grant said, confused.

"No," I repeated. "I won't."

"What do you mean, you won't?" he said, baffled. "When was the last time I asked you for anything? All I want is a simple email. Something that will take zero effort on your part but could save me from jail. You can't manage that much for me? After you took millions of dollars of my money?"

"Our money," I said. "We were married nineteen years, and you hid it from me. It was illegal. And wrong. And for the record, the last thing you asked me for was a divorce, and I gave you that. I don't owe you anything else. Goodbye, Grant."

I pressed the red disconnect button with one trembling finger, then kept pressing it until my whole finger turned white.

Gigi flung herself at me, wrapping me into a tight embrace. "My brave, sweet girl," she said. "You are not his pawn or entertainment source anymore. You are a strong, independent, vibrant, beautiful woman." She released me and cackled. "And you told him to stick it!"

Tears blurred my eyes as belated panic seized my chest. "Thank you," I croaked. "I'm just sorry I let him make me forget who I was for so long."

She stepped back to press soft palms to my cheeks. "You remember now, and life is good."

I nodded, feeling my smile widen. "It is."

A knock on the glass door at my back drew our attention to a Lexi-shaped shadow inside my shop.

Gigi opened the door, and Lexi bounced into the bakery.

"It's closing time," she said, hugging Gigi, then turning her smile on me. "I counted down the register and locked up. Clyde's waiting in the window display, pouncing at passersby."

"Thanks," I said, dropping a kiss on Gigi's cheek. "I'll see you tomorrow?"

"You betcha," she said.

I smiled at her once more, then left Lexi behind, oohing and aahing at the changes inside the bakery.

I couldn't spare another minute. I had a hot dinner date to attend.

I dropped Clyde at home for his dinner and headed over to Mason's house alone. I'd changed into a soft pair of blue jeans and a cream knit sweater with tan booties. It was my attempt at appearing cuddly but fashionable. My version of sweatpants and a hoodie, which I couldn't pull off without looking dumpy or ill.

Mason met me at the door to his houseboat in bare feet, jeans and a gray t-shirt that fit him magnificently. "Hey," he said.

"Hi." I stepped inside, inhaling the comforting scent of his shampoo and cologne as I passed.

Mason's houseboat was older than either of us and still dressed in its original glory. Lots of tan and brown everywhere with a few punches of orange and gold for fun. I had dreams of giving the place a complete makeover in shades of gray with highlights of white and icy blue. I didn't bother bringing the ideas up for fear he'd never invite me back. Mason was resistant to making things too nice or comfortable, probably because someone other than me might drop by unannounced or, worse, want to stay for a visit. So far he'd avoided both by treating his home's location as if it were a state secret.

But it was only a matter of time before some well-meaning folks found him and told everyone they knew.

Meanwhile, I'd been playing the long game in regard to his outdated décor, leaving things behind about once a week. Like a nice hand towel for the bathroom or a set of ivory bookends for his shelves. Smuggling decorative pillows and a nice throw blanket for his couch would require an epic ninja move and a massive handbag, but I was working on it.

On days I didn't bring anything to leave behind, I casually tucked something ugly out of sight, into a cabinet or drawer.

Because who needed a ceramic ash tray anymore? Not anyone I knew. And dogs should never play poker, not even to pose for a painting.

"How was work?" Mason asked, locking up behind me, then shuffling to the kitchen.

"Good. You?"

He grunted. "You've really got to love people to be a small-town sheriff," he said.

I smiled. "I knew you loved people."

"Incorrect." He pulled a large tossed salad from the fridge and placed it between us on the counter.

I set my purse and coat on one tall bar stool and hiked myself onto the other.

"That's why I made a great homicide detective in Cleveland," he said. "I didn't have to make nice with anyone. My subjects were dead, and my suspects didn't need a friendly face. No one needed a friendly face. In fact, my expression alone used to make it clear I wasn't sociable and didn't want to be. Down here I scowl at someone, and they stop to ask me if I'm okay or if there's anything they can do to help."

I laughed.

He frowned.

"Are you okay?" I asked.

"Funny."

"I mean it," I said. "You seem more prickly than usual. What's up?"

Mason dished out two salads. "I've got a casserole in the oven from a lady who I helped haul groceries to her car. She dropped it off at the station, and our freezer there is full of similar casseroles, so I had to bring this one home."

I smiled. "You're such a nice man, helping ladies with their groceries."

He passed me a fork, then took a seat at my side. "I have a story for you."

I suppressed the urge to clap. Sharing any kind of information usually went against his instincts, but I'd asked him to try, and for the past few months, he had been. In return for that trust, I was lowering my guard as well. "Okay. Hit me."

"I stopped by the fruit-and-veggie stand in Cromwell on my way home so I could pick up all this," he said, motioning to the salad. "And there was a commotion."

My ears perked. "What kind of commotion?"

"A Cromwell police officer was arguing with your friend, Louisa, and her ex-boyfriend, who'd apparently gotten into a spat over their chicken."

"Thelma," I said.

His eyes sparkled with humor. "Right. So, the former couple was arguing, and the police officer was just making it all worse. Then he told Louisa to calm down."

I bristled.

"Yeah, she had the same reaction," Mason said, a smile tugging the corner of his mouth. "So she told him if he spoke down to her again she'd tell his mama."

I set my fork aside, too delighted to eat.

"Then the ex-boyfriend says, why don't we all calm down?"

I snorted.

Mason's eyes were wide as he barreled ahead, fully entertained. "Now, there's a crowd, and I just want to pay for my produce and go home."

"You were shopping?" I said. "While they argued?"

"I was trying. There wasn't anything I could do about the fight, and Louisa clearly had it covered. The cop tried to come back at her, but she stamped her little black shoe and told him he'd best get out of her sight, because she was fixin' to pinch his head off." He barked out a laugh. "I don't even know what that means, but people laughed, and the cop turned red."

I went back to my salad, trying to imagine the scene playing out. "I guess Louisa isn't as sweet and helpless as she looks. Good for her."

"Well, she certainly scared her ex," Mason said. "Or embarrassed him well enough, because he left. The cop stuck around to tell folks there wasn't anything to see, and a white-haired woman selling jams said that was true because Louisa had sorted it." Mason's smile grew. "Then the cop noticed me watching, and before I could pretend I didn't see anything, Louisa walked up to me and started talking. There's no way that guy didn't realize I got the full show of his incompetence. Embarrassing."

As the county sheriff, Mason and his deputies were Bliss's only source of law enforcement, but they retained jurisdiction over Cromwell as well.

"That's what happens when everyone knows everyone," I said. "They get in one another's business and threaten to call your mama."

The oven beeped, and Mason rose to claim the casserole. "This place is surreal. Oh, man, that smells good. Remind me to thank this woman if I ever see her again."

I paused, fork halfway to my lips. "You're practically guaranteed to see her again, and you're supposed to write a thank-you note."

He set the casserole on the stove to cool. "No, she was thanking me for the help with her groceries."

"And you need to thank her for the food. You need to tell her it was delicious," I said.

His brows dipped low. "Am I supposed to thank everyone who's brought me food since I got here?"

I nodded, suddenly horrified he hadn't. "Didn't you?"

"Of course not. I'd have to write notes to half the town," he complained. "I don't even know the names of everyone who brought me dinner. I couldn't find them to thank them if I tried."

"Please," I said dryly and rolling my eyes. "You're the sheriff. You can find an address on anyone you want, and I can tell you who they are."

He squinted. "How? Is there some kind of welcome-wagon roster I don't know about?"

"That's not a bad idea, but no. I can tell by their casserole dish. Did you keep the dishes?"

"I didn't throw them away," he said, as if that would be ridiculous.

I climbed off my stool, opening and closing my hand in the universal sign for gimmee.

He opened a cupboard door to expose piles of bakeware. "The freezer's full too."

I grabbed the magnetic pad of paper and pen I'd left on his refrigerator last week and started to write. "Susie Jo Huffstetter." I peeled the page off and set it inside the top dish, a clear glass pie plate. "LuAnn McGonnel," I said, sliding the second sheet into the same piece of antique Fiestaware I'd seen at every town event in my life. "Mrs. Thatcher. Mr. and Mrs. Simmons. Janice Hartman."

"How are you doing that?" he asked, arms crossed and expression hard.

"I know the dishes," I said. "Most folks use the same pieces over and over as their go-tos. They save those just for delivering meals to others or attending events. Something nice enough to be seen in public and represent your kitchen but not so nice that you won't get over losing it. LuAnn's antiques are an exception."

Mason watched as I picked my way through the rest of the dishes. He turned to serve the casserole when I opened his fridge.

"I'll bring you some thank-you cards tomorrow. We can fill them out together," I said. "I don't suppose you remember what was in any of these?"

He set our meals on the island. "No. Do you want to eat on the deck? It's a clear night, and I got new heaters out there."

"Yes, please." I slid my coat back on, then grabbed my plate and followed Mason outside.

Beyond the wall of windows in his living room was a wide deck with a currently retracted awning.

Mason fired up the space heaters. He turned the lights off inside before taking the seat beside me at his table set, leaving us to dine by moonlight and a set of flameless candles on a silver tray. I'd dropped the centerpiece off on New Year's Eve.

"Your turn," he said, digging into a mound of chicken tetrazzini. "How was your day after I left?"

I forked a piece of chicken and a mushroom, considering where to begin. My gut told me I should say everything was fine, then change the subject, but Mason and I were trying to learn to be normal, open people who had authentic real-talk conversations. Plus, he'd already shared about his day. "Grant called again. I was with Gigi, so I answered."

Mason stopped chewing, and his eyes met mine.

"It was uncomfortable, and I panicked a little at first," I admitted. "Then I told him if he called again I would file harassment charges." I smiled, feeling both awkward and empowered.

"Good for you," Mason said, sounding as if he meant it. "You should be proud. That wasn't easy."

"Thanks." The mileage between Grant in Atlanta and me in Bliss helped ease my anxiety.

Mason set his fork aside and leaned in my direction. "Can I say I'm proud of you or is that too proprietary? I know you aren't a child, or mine to take pride in, but I don't think there's a better word for what I'm feeling."

My heart swelled, and I leaned in his direction too. "That feels really good to hear, actually," I whispered.

Mason grinned. "You know what else feels really good?" he asked, his mouth drifting closer.

A small, distant voice interrupted the silence of the night, wrecking our moment.

We straightened and turned to see flashlight beams sweeping the ground near the road. Voices reached our ears in nearly inaudible bursts, growing louder as the group came slowly closer.

"What is that?" I asked, confused.

Mason stood and moved to the railing. "It looks like a search party."

CHAPTER FOUR

Mason and I hurried down the dock to the land beyond, hoping to find out who was missing and how we could help. "I hope it's not a kid," Mason said. "I hate when it's a kid."

My stomach dropped at the reminder he'd been through things I couldn't imagine before moving to my town. "Me too," I said, suspecting the odds of finding a child uninjured after dark would be significantly lower than the odds of finding an uninjured adult.

The group stilled as we approached, their beams falling to their feet and their voices quieting.

"Hey!" Mason called, towing me along more quickly. "Everything okay?"

The silhouettes became four men as we drew near, and I noticed they were all in odd, old-timey clothing, circa *Little House on the Prairie.*

"Sheriff," one man said, stepping forward to greet us. The hint of an Irish accent touched his words. "Sorry to disturb you so late."

I checked the time on my phone. It was only 8:25.

"It's no trouble, Eli," Mason said. "We were eating dinner and saw the lights."

Eli swung his troubled gaze to me. "Sorry to interrupt your dinner, ma'am."

"Bonnie," I said, lifting my hand in a hip-high wave, introducing myself when Mason failed to do it for me. "Who's missing? We want to help."

Eli nodded, and a mass of clouds passed away from the moon, allowing its silver glow to illuminate his chiseled jaw and long, straight nose. His eyes were light, but not blue, maybe hazel like mine. The moon was bright enough to show he'd be gorgeous regardless of his eye color, the night still dark enough to cast an air of mystery.

I puckered my lips to whistle, but remembered myself and pressed them flat instead.

"We're turning back," he said. "We were looking for a friend's pet, but there's no way it could've gotten this far. We'll start over at ground zero and fan out in another direction."

"Dog?" Mason asked, relief coloring the word.

"Nah," Eli said.

I mentally compared the two men, while the rest of the rescue party stared into the shadows, turning in small circles, flashlights hunting through the night.

Eli was tall and broad, muscular where Mason was lean and wiry. Eli had the chest and arms of a man accustomed to manual labor. Apparently a lot of it.

Mason looked at me. "Did you just whistle?"

"Hmm?" I asked, brows climbing. "I don't think so."

Mason made a face at me that suggested I'd gone around the bend, then turned back to Eli.

"A hen," Eli said, completing his answer to Mason's question. "Tan and white. About yay big." He tucked the light beneath his crooked arm to mime the approximate size of the missing fowl.

Mason stiffened slightly at my side, probably imagining a chicken lurking in the night, waiting to attack. "You don't mean Louisa Eggers's pet?"

My heart sprinted and chest tightened at the awful thought. "Thelma's missing?"

Eli scrunched his handsome face. "You know Thelma?"

"You know Louisa?" I asked. Suddenly the men's odd attire made more sense. These must've been men from her little cottagecore community. "You're Eli-Eli," I said, his name registering for the first time. He wasn't a farmhand; he was a blacksmith and a lumberjack.

"Yes?" he said, unsure. "Have we met?"

"No." I shook my head. "But Louisa mentioned you when I saw her earlier today, and I just put two and two together."

"How long has Thelma been missing?" Mason asked, rightfully keeping us on track.

"We're not sure," Eli said. "Louisa went to the farmers' market and ran some errands. When she got home and settled, she went to feed the hens, but Thelma was gone."

I looked to Mason. "You saw her arguing with Ben at the farmers' market." They'd fought over Thelma, and Ben left first.

Mason nodded, probably thinking the same thing.

"He could've gone to her place and taken the chicken," I said.

Mason scratched his cheek. "I should probably call the local PD."

"They don't care," Eli said. "They do what they can to avoid our community. We're going to need some evidence before we accuse one of the townies of a crime." Eli searched my face while I frowned at the word *townies*. "What did Louisa say about me?" he asked.

I didn't know how to answer that, so I looked at Mason.

He crossed his arms, still watching Eli. "Do you have any idea where Louisa is now?"

A white-haired fellow patted Eli on the shoulder. "We're going to head back and keep looking. Let you handle this."

"I'll catch up," Eli called after them. When he returned his attention to Mason, his jaw had tensed. "Louisa also thought Ben took the hen, or set her lose while Louisa was out, because if he couldn't have Thelma, no one could. So she went to confront him while we started looking."

I groaned, and Mason echoed the sentiment. "Have you spoken with her since she left? Do you know for sure Thelma wasn't at Ben's place?"

Eli nodded. "Louisa called to say he wasn't home, and there weren't any signs of Thelma. She was going to try to catch up with him, check his usual hangouts. We had to start looking. It was already dark and chickens aren't smart. Plus they have no way to defend themselves against predators." Anguish relaxed his features by a fraction. "I'd hate to think of what losing Thelma would do to Louisa."

"Me too," I agreed.

"I really need to find her." He looked over his shoulder in the direction his men had gone. "I'm going to catch up with them and keep looking. Enjoy your dinner. Give me a call if you spot a hen running around?"

Mason offered his hand in a goodbye shake. "Will do."

We turned back toward the boat, but I'd lost my appetite.

"I don't like this," Mason said.

"A chicken on the loose in the dark?" I teased, squeezing his fingers with mine.

"Don't even joke about that. I meant Louisa hunting down her ex. A lot of people saw them arguing today, including a member of the police department. I don't under-stand the dynamics at play here yet, but it could be bad if he accuses her of something while there's no one around to take her side."

Another thought slipped into mind, and my steps slowed. "How do you know Eli?" Mason had greeted him by name on sight, and he'd agreed to call him without having to ask for his number.

Mason slid his eyes my way without missing a step. "From town."

"But he lives in Louisa's community."

"Yeah." He looked at me, then back to the lake and his boat as we approached the dock. "But we both live in Cromwell."

I squinted up at him as my intuition itched, then lost my train of thought when I looked forward again. Something light-colored caught my eye in the water near a patch of tall grasses. "Is that—" I said, imagining poor Thelma drowned or entrapped by a snake. "Do you see that?"

"Yep."

We broke into a run together, but Mason pulled immediately ahead, eating up the distance with his ridiculously long strides. He stopped short a few feet from the water's edge and thrust his arms out at his sides to stop me from getting in front of him.

"Wait," he said. "Back up." He pulled his cell phone from his pocket and initiated the flashlight app, then pointed the beam at what I hoped wasn't a chicken. A small curse followed.

"What is it?" I asked, afraid to know, but needing to ask. "Is it Thelma?"

Mason lowered his arm and wrapped it around my back instead, tugging me close. "I've got to call this in. We're probably contaminating a crime scene."

I stared at the light sweeping the water's edge while he turned his phone around to dial. A man floated facedown less than three yards away, a nasty gash on his head. "That's not Thelma."

"No," Mason said. "It's Ben Reid. Louisa's ex."

An hour later, the night was lit up like a Hollywood set, courtesy of multiple megawatt lights on tripods and a number of emergency vehicles, headlights pointed at the lake.

A bevy of first responders had apparently shown up to stand around and watch the area, since none seemed to actually be doing anything.

The coroner had trudged into the water wearing rubber waders and was working with a team to relocate the body to a white sheet on solid ground.

It was strange to know this lifeless form had dated Louisa. He wore what I recognized to be two-hundred-dollar skinny jeans and a sixty-five-dollar t-shirt. Grant had plenty of both brands back in Atlanta. The easily recognizable logos were displayed in plain sight, across the pocket, just the way people who loved high-end things preferred. His leather boat shoes and designer dress socks with eggplant emojis completed the ensemble.

I sat on the icy grass in my upcycled sweater and vintage jeans, arms wrapped around myself to defend against the biting air. My teeth chattered slightly from the cold but also from the desperate concern about what all this could mean.

Where were Thelma and Louisa? Was Louisa missing now too? Had she been with Ben when the killer arrived? Had she been harmed, or worse, when Ben was taken to the lake?

I dialed Louisa for the dozenth time and said another prayer that she would answer as onlookers trickled in. Folks brought steaming disposable cups for the first responders. They passed them out, then lingered on the outskirts of the chaos, drawn to the scene by carousels of emergency lighting in the otherwise clear night sky.

A moment later, like each time before, my call went to voicemail.

"Hey," a low male voice caught my attention before I noticed Eli headed my way. "May I join you?" he asked.

"Of course."

He lowered himself to my side, casting a thankful look at me before turning his attention to the body being bagged by the coroner. "I don't suppose you've heard from Louisa," he said, a note of fear mixing with the light accent I'd noticed before.

"She's not answering."

"For me either." "Any news on Thelma?" I asked.

Eli shook his head. "No, ma'am."

I released a ragged sigh. "I just met Louisa a few months ago. She's a friend of a friend. I helped her choose some dresses for her next poultry showing. I'm going to help her set up her soufflé stand when she's ready. How do you know her?"

Eli frowned. "We both live in the Meadowbrook community."

"She mentioned that." I'd been hoping for something more to work with. "Your accent suggests you aren't originally from Georgia," I said, offering an encouraging smile. "Where were you before Meadowbrook?"

"Around," he said. "Before that, Wicklow."

"Ireland?"

He nodded, but didn't elaborate or look at me again.

"I have some family in Wicklow," I said. "It's small. I don't think I've ever known anyone else with people there."

He didn't respond.

Across the grass, a pair of uniformed cops marched in Mason's direction, and he turned to frown in response. Their lips moved, as did their hands. First the uniformed officers. Then Mason.

"You never told me what Louisa said about me," Eli said.

I turned to look at him, hoping there was a nice reason he wanted to know.

He kept his eyes on Mason and the officers, staring so intently I suspected he could read lips.

"She said you're a lumberjack and a blacksmith," I told him. "And that you step in as needed to keep the peace. Also that you are kind."

His frown deepened. "I'm not kind," he said, turning the full force of his broody stare on me.

I felt the heat of his response radiate across the space between us, and my mouth opened, but words failed.

"If I was a kind man," he said, the gentle tenor turning to a growl. "I wouldn't have wished Ben Reid dead."

Someone cleared their throat, and I looked up to find Mason and one of the uniformed officers approaching.

Eli winced.

The officer widened his stance and set his hands on his hips. He was half a foot shorter than Mason, and his narrow chest and shoulders made him seem even smaller beside the frowning sheriff.

Mason sucked his teeth and focused on me. "I'm afraid I'm going to be here a while," he said. "Cromwell PD has asked for assistance from the sheriff's department."

Eli stretched onto his feet, looking Mason squarely in the eye while wholly ignoring the other officer. "Any word on Louisa?"

"Not yet," Mason said.

In the distance, a car door slammed, and Louisa's voice echoed through the cool night. "Eli!"

She ran across the field in our direction, dodging authorities and ignoring everything except the man at my side. "Eli!"

We turned in stunned silence to watch her approach.

She thrust herself into his arms. "I'm so sorry," she cried. "I lost track of time and my phone died. I was looking for Thelma until I just couldn't go on anymore. I saw the emergency lights, and someone told me you were headed this way when they saw you last. I thought—" She pulled back and looked up at him, then stepped away, smoothing her dress. "I thought you were hurt."

Eli stared back, his arms still lifted slightly from his sides, as if her hug had startled him.

"Miss Eggers," the uniformed cop drawled. "You want to tell me where you've been for the past two hours?"

She blinked several times. "Looking for Thelma. We all were."

"Anyone who can confirm your whereabouts?" he asked.

Louisa looked to Eli, then me, confusion wrinkling her brow. "What do you mean? Why is it anyone's business where I've been? Someone stole my chicken. I told you that, and you told me finding livestock wasn't a police officer's job."

"Miss Eggers," he repeated. "I'm going to have to ask you to—"

"Do not tell me to calm down again," she said, raising a finger in warning. "Thelma is missing!"

"And Ben Reid is dead," he said. "So I'm going to ask you again, and you can answer me here or down at the station. Is there anyone who can confirm your whereabouts for the past two hours?"

Louisa stumbled back a step, seeming to take note of the larger picture for the first time. Seeming to ask herself, if Eli wasn't hurt, then what exactly was going on here?

Another cop car arrived, and two women got out. One in a Cromwell PD uniform. The other in long corduroy skirt and sweater.

The woman in the sweater had straight dark hair that reached her waist and eyes that narrowed as she approached. "Arrest her!" she called, pointing a finger at Louisa. "She threatened to kill Ben, and now she'd done it! Over a stupid chicken!"

Louisa gasped at the last part.

Eli set a protective hand on Louisa's shoulder. "You can't go around throwing accusations like that, Mary. We've talked about this."

"Then you did it," she snapped. "You'd do anything for her." Mary nearly spit the last word, and Eli dropped his hand away from Louisa.

Mason raised his palms and dragged his gaze from face to face. "Just a minute. You're going to have to catch me up. I'm Sheriff Wright. Who are you?"

"I'm Mary Acres," the other simply dressed woman stated. "I'm Ben's girlfriend, and I want her arrested!"

"Knock that off," I said, pulling Louisa to my side, unwilling to see her battered any further. "Stop being ugly." It was obvious to anyone with eyes that Louisa had no idea what was going on when she'd arrived, and the announcement of her ex's death had nearly doubled her over with shock.

Mason stepped forward, redirecting Mary's attention.

I concentrated on poor Louisa and the awful night she was clearly having. "I will help you get to the bottom of this," I promised. "Just breathe. We'll find Thelma and figure the rest out in time. Okay?"

Mason shot me a sidelong glance.

Louisa nodded as she began to sob.

CHAPTER FIVE

I woke early the next morning to Clyde's teeth on my toes. I'd been able to ignore the headbutts, and I'd retracted my limbs beneath my blankets like a turtle, but he'd followed.

"Clyde!" I scolded, sitting upright and squinting against the rays of morning sunlight invading my room.

I really needed something heavier and more light-absorbent for the bedroom windows.

"Meow," Clyde lamented. "Meow. Meow. Meow!"

"I'm coming. Jeez."

I set my bare feet on the cold floor and made a mental note to find a rug for under the bed while I was shopping for curtains. Then, I headed for the kitchen.

I filled Clyde's bowl, got my morning coffee going, and left Clyde to eat while I went to get dressed. I selected my favorite black slacks and cream blouse as memories of the night before came flooding back. By the time I'd fastened a matching pinstriped bowtie around Clyde's neck, my mind was in a full spin.

Louisa's ex had drowned in Lake Cromwell. Thelma was

missing. And some woman from Louisa's sweet little community had shown up at the crime scene accusing Louisa, and possibly Eli, of the murder. Only a few minutes before that, Eli had admitted to wishing Ben dead. And a few hours earlier still, local cops and Mason had witnessed Louisa and Ben arguing publicly.

I pressed my hands to my head and hurried to the kitchen for coffee.

Ten minutes later, I was cruising toward town.

Normally, I'd have spent time curled in a blanket on my patio with a cup of coffee before work. Impersonating a burrito while enjoying the fog as it hovered over the lake in my backyard had become a beloved part of my morning routine. But today there was a woman to comfort, a chicken to find, and a murder to solve.

I knew it was wrong to feel so jazzed when a person's death was involved, but adrenaline raced through my veins nonetheless.

I motored into town, recounting the night's events to Clyde, who'd been asleep and in no mood to listen when I'd arrived home the night before. "Thankfully neither Louisa nor Eli were arrested," I said, "but I don't like Mary, and I'm not impressed with the cops over there. It's a good thing they have Mason to help."

Clyde stretched and shook his head hard, as if something had given him a tickle.

I smiled.

Folks were out in droves as I approached the town square. Some were picking up coffees and pastries to start their days. It wouldn't be long before they could stop at Oh, My Goodies to see Gigi for those things, and I couldn't wait.

The space outside my store was open, and I slid my white Volkswagen Cabriolet convertible against the curb. "It's going to be a good day," I told Clyde as I dragged his carrier across the console, then beeped the doors locked and strode through the brisk morning air.

Our town square was actually a large grassy oval, which had once served as a football field. Today it held a half dozen mossy oaks, flagstone paths, benches and an octagonal gazebo. Roads formed a ring around it with shops on each side. Bless Her Heart included.

I hopped onto the sidewalk in time to see Gigi poke her head out of the bakery door.

"Come," she said, waving me toward her. "You've got to see this."

I hurried in her direction, putting thoughts of the murder in Cromwell behind me. I'd never be able to help with a crime in another town, I told myself, not for the first time. Or the tenth. My life was too busy. And Cromwell was the enemy. Blissers could see me crossing the line and think I'd defected. Plus, there'd be no way to hide my involvement from Mason since he was helping on the case. And he really hated when I got involved.

So I definitely wouldn't.

Of course, I could still help with Louisa's soufflé stand. And no one could fault me for visiting her if I had a legitimate and business-related reason. While I was there I might as well see what I could do to comfort her, and maybe learn a little more about the missing chicken.

Gigi stepped aside to let me enter Oh My Goodies, and I marveled.

She'd scrubbed the place spotless and framed a Good Luck Falls calendar on the wall near the checkout.

"Nice." I grinned. Mason was going to hate that when it was his month.

"Display cases are coming today," she said. "And the carpenter. I think I'll be ready in time for Valentine's Day. Now all I need to do is put the announcement in the paper.

"Are you having a grand opening?" I asked. "Something official and splashy?"

"Boy am I," she said. "I've been working on my gimmicks. Blind Date with a Pie," she said. "I'll box a bunch of pies and sell them with no labels. Get it? Blind dates. I'm also making special Single Ladies Pastries for the women who plan to enjoy the evening alone and treat herself. And I'm selling chocolates and cookies in How Much Do You Love Her quantities. No one will want to buy only a half dozen. They'll look uninvested. So, those are guaranteed to go like hotcakes. And I've hired a jug band for entertainment."

I laughed. "Clever. I love seeing you so happy, and everything sounds great. Your grand opening is sure to be a hit."

"I couldn't have done it without you," she said, looking softer and smaller than I was accustomed. "I don't think I can ever properly thank you."

"I'm glad I could help."

I'd been happy to finance the bakery with some of my divorce settlement, and I had plans to make more differences like this one all over town.

"I'll leave it to you when I go," Gigi said, turning her eyes skyward and signing the cross.

"Stop it. You're going to live forever, so there's no need to think like that."

She raised and dropped one hand. "I'm just saying is all."

I shook my head, unwilling to think of losing her. My heart couldn't take it.

"Did Grant bother you anymore after you left here yesterday?" Gigi asked, thankfully changing the subject.

"No." I paused, realizing she had no idea what I'd been through last night.

The invisible line between Bliss and Cromwell was like a giant cone of silence or a magical barrier of some kind.

She dipped her chin, satisfied. "Good. What will you do if he calls again today?"

"I don't know," I admitted. I could ask Mason for help, but I didn't want to keep interacting with Grant. I just wanted him to go away. "Maybe I'll change my number." That would be easier, and less humbling than asking my boyfriend to help me file harassment charges against my annoying ex-husband. "I'll have to think about it a little more."

"That's fair," Gigi said. "Avoidance always works like a charm."

I couldn't tell if she was joking, but she wasn't wrong, at least as far as my experience. "Avoidance is my super power," I assured her.

"Any chance you're going to book club this week?" she asked.

"I hadn't thought about it. Why? Are you?"

A handful of Gigi's friends met monthly at the local book shop, What the Dickens. Gigi and Mama had been taking me there my entire life. And I'd always liked the woman who'd run it, Hazel. Her granddaughter, Liz, had taken over after her passing. I liked Liz too, but I rarely attended book club.

"I'm going for sure," Gigi said. "You should come. Sutton's in town for a visit, and she wants to go. You know," she said, eyes widening a bit dramatically. "If you have time, you could pick up the books for us and grab one for yourself."

I shot her a droll look. "Oh, gee. Can I?"

"Yes. I'd appreciate it. I'm going to be too busy to finish the story, but I like to support Liz and see the ladies."

"I'll get your books."

"Join us," she said. "You'll have a good time, and Sutton would love to see you. She's staying with me if you want to stop by my place later."

Sutton was an old friend of Gigi's who lived in Virginia now but visited often. She was also a bit of a self-proclaimed mystic, who dressed like a hippie and thought she could talk to plants and animals.

"I'll try to come to book club," I said.

I planted a goodbye kiss on Gigi's cheek and headed for the door. "Tell Sutton I'm glad she's here."

I moved onto the sidewalk with a smile. Sutton had once given me a small potted plant named Judy, who she'd sworn would protect me, and strangely, it kind of had.

So, it looked like I'd be attending book club.

CHAPTER SIX

What the Dickens didn't open for another hour, so Clyde and I went to Bless Her Heart instead. Thanks to Lexi's hard work at closing the night before, there wasn't much to do.

All my prettiest pastel items were featured in displays, interspersed with gratuitous amounts of Valentine-themed décor. Soft aqua bookcases with pretty cloth-covered tomes. Pale-pink and lavender throw pillows, a plethora of red dresses, handbags and shoes. Even the vases on my counter, filled with bouquets from my folks' farm, were made of pale-green milk glass and tied with heart-covered ribbons.

Clyde pounced on something near the chairs outside my dressing rooms, then darted into the window display.

I flipped the sign on my shop door to OPEN, then went to hunt for a container of recent donations in the crowded storeroom. I kept my ears open for customers as I searched. It wasn't long before Clyde joined me, prowling through the congested space and pawing select boxes wildly for no reason I could see. He nosed along the folded flaps and dragged his cheek over the corners. Fully delighted to explore the room I usually kept closed.

"Any chance you can put some of that enthusiasm to use helping me find the donations from the theater troop?" I asked. "The box said 'costume design' on one side and smelled a little like Gigi's crawl space."

The bells over my front door jingled, and I ushered Clyde into the hallway, pulling the storeroom door shut behind me. With a little luck, Lexi would know where I should look next.

"Welcome to Bless Her Heart," I called, hustling back to the sales floor.

Lexi squinted up from behind the counter, lifting her crossbody bag over her head. Long dark hair fell over her shoulders and splayed across her forehead in a spray of grown-out bangs. "Good morning," she said with a yawn. She tucked her bag on a shelf beneath the register and turned to rest against the desk. "I'm so not a morning person."

I smiled. "In less than two weeks, we'll have Blissful Bean coffee for sale again next door. For now, I can start a pot of store-bought if you're interested."

She headed to the refreshments table and lifted the pot. "I've got this. I'm the one who can't keep my eyes open. Speaking of Gigi's bakery, can you believe how good it looks in there?"

"It's going to be a showstopper," I agreed.

Over-the-top displays of fancy weren't the typical aesthetic in Bliss, so Gigi's bakery was going against the norm, but I was confident folks would love it. And when everyone understood how nice it was to feel pampered, the bar would raise for the rest of us.

Thankfully, I already had a delightfully enchanting shop.

Clyde leaped onto the counter and made a proud yowling sound. I turned to see what he was bragging about. Typically he saved that particular noise for unfortunate field mice and unsuspecting sparrows.

"Aw," Lexi said. "He has a feather. I think it's one of Thelma's. I must've missed it when I vacuumed last night."

I moved around the counter to get a better look. "I think you're right."

"He liked her," she said. "They were so cute together."

Clyde would probably like to eat her, I thought, but that didn't seem proper to point out. "I wonder what she thought of him?" I asked instead.

Lexi shrugged. "Thelma is so used to people and other animals, she probably assumed he was another friend."

I grimaced. That wasn't great news. "She went missing last night," I said.

Hopefully, she hadn't walked up to a fox thinking they could be friends.

Lexi's eyes widened, and I filled her in on what I knew. She began to text Louisa as I spoke, letting her know she wanted to help however she could.

When I finished the story, and we both had a cup of coffee in hand, I changed the subject to the other thing on my mind. "Have you seen the box of donations we got from that theater troop last month?"

She sipped thoughtfully from her cup, eyelids fluttering as the caffeine began its work. "I think we moved it to the storage unit. Why?"

"Oh, right."

I'd rented a small storage unit in town to help manage the incredible amount of donations I received. Now that Lexi had said it, I vaguely remembered including the theater stuff with a load headed that way.

"I thought Louisa would like the old-fashioned dresses," I said, belatedly answering her question. "And some of the set props might work for her soufflé stand's décor."

Lexi smiled. "Smart."

"I have my moments."

Lexi's smile fell, and she looked to the door before setting her coffee aside. "Can I talk to you about something?"

"Sure," I said, sensing sudden tension in the room. "What's up?"

She tugged her ear and crossed her arms. "I've been thinking for a while about taking a big step, and I want to get your thoughts. I tried talking to my mom, but she blew me off, and my siblings think I'm being ridiculous."

"Okay," I said cautiously. "What is it?"

"I want to go to college," she said, expression hard, as if prepared for some sort of negative retort.

I nearly collapsed in relief, thankful she didn't want to meet a man she'd met on the internet at a private location, or invest in an overseas financial scam of some sort. "College?"

"I know it's stupid to think I can do it. No one in my family has ever gone. I swear I don't think I'm some special unicorn or that I'm better than anyone else. I just want to learn stuff, and I think I'd like taking classes. It was fun learning about merchandising and marketing from you, about flowers and science from your folks, and baking from Gigi. And I want to learn more. I hated high school, but working here got me thinking about what else might be out there for me. Not that I don't love this," she quickly added. "I do. Right now. But what about when I'm twenty? Or thirty?"

I felt the familiar prick of pride in my eyes and worked to straighten my expression.

"Are you about to cry?" she asked, tightening her arms over her chest. "Did I say something wrong?"

"Goodness, no." I cleared my throat. "Lexi. I think going to college would be an amazing adventure for you. You're one of the smartest people I know, and you will succeed at whatever you do."

"Stop," she said, frowning. "I barely graduated high school. I don't expect to do great or change the world. I just want…I don't know…something more."

I frowned back at her, hung up on the possibility she'd failed at anything. "How hard did you try in high school?"

"What?" she stalled, having obviously heard my question. "I don't know."

I raised my brows and waited. "You say you barely graduated, but how hard did you try?"

"A little," she said. Her gaze dropped to her feet. "Not a lot, I guess. I didn't understand the point of putting in a ton of effort when I was just going to wind up waiting tables like my mom and taking care of my younger siblings while she worked opposite shifts from me."

I held my tongue when she paused to chew her lip, clearly having more to say.

"I thought about stealing that prom dress."

My brows rose, and I inched closer, stopping to lean against my counter. "The one I traded you for a few hours of work here?"

She bit her lip again. "It was something I thought my mom would've done at my age, so she couldn't be mad if I got caught. I think that was the day I first realized I'd been using her as an excuse for most of my crappy choices. Then you were so nice to me. You offered me a job in trade for the dress when you knew I couldn't afford it. Which was ridiculous of you, by the way. I could've been a terrible person. I could've never come back to work off the payment. Or I could've come back and stolen everything in sight."

I gave her my best be-serious face.

She smiled. "Okay, maybe not me, but someone could've, and you didn't know me. I still don't know what made me come in here that day, or why I thought there was a chance I could afford to go to prom."

"I do," I said, offering an encouraging smile. "You have two things a lot of people don't. Dreams and hope."

She lifted her eyes to meet mine again. "I've been thoroughly and repeatedly warned that both are dangerous and stupid."

"Probably by people who've had their hopes and dreamed dashed. But even that isn't a reason to give up."

Lexi looked away again.

"If you want to go to college, I think that is exactly what you should do," I said. "Register for a class or two and see for yourself. Take courses online from home. Attend locally. Get a student loan, move to another state and live on campus. However you do it, I know you'll love college. And I think you might get straight As."

Lexi frowned. Her face crunched and twisted, then the tears began to fall.

"Come here." I wrapped her in a hug and set my chin on her shoulder. "I'm really proud of you," I whispered. "It's a big and scary deal to shake things up like this. To push and challenge yourself. To go after what you want. But I believe you can do anything. And you won't know unless you try."

Her arms tightened around me, and I wondered how long it'd been since anyone had really hugged her. When she backed away, I saw a nervous kid behind a lifetime of emotional armor. "Will you help me with the paperwork?" she asked, struggling to clear her throat. "Most of it's online, but there's a lot, and I don't know where to start. I've already missed this semester, so I have to apply for summer or fall. My high school counselor thought I might qualify for financial aid, but I don't know where to begin."

"I can help you with all of that," I said, already wondering how difficult it would be to start an annual scholarship fund for local high school seniors. A thousand dollars a year to a handful of applicants could make an enormous difference in a lot of lives.

Lexi wiped the corners of her eyes discreetly and went back to her coffee. "Cool."

"Cool," I agreed. "I need to run out for a little while. I'm going to the storage unit to look for that box, then to What the Dickens to pick up this month's book club book for Gigi. Do you need anything while I'm gone?"

Lexi shook her head. "I'm good. I'll hold down the fort."

I grabbed my purse, coat and keys. "Text if you change your mind or anything comes up."

"Bonnie?" she asked, stopping me as I set a hand on the door. "Do you think Louisa will still get to open her soufflé stand? What if she's arrested? Or spends all her savings on a lawyer?"

I released a deep sigh. I'd wondered the same things and appreciated her concern for a friend. "I'm going to do what I can to make sure the bad stuff doesn't happen. I'll keep you in the loop."

I marched into the biting air, cursing winter for its audacity. "Why do people live up north?" I muttered to myself, unable to imagine choosing to spend three months fighting snow and ice. Those folks would probably think of today's forecasted high of 47 as a winter heatwave. And the current barely-above-freezing temperature as no big deal.

Further evidence all that frost affected their brains.

I halted my internal rant when a man I recognized as Travis Eggers appeared on the square. Travis was Louisa's uncle, and we'd met last summer when he purchased a local botanical garden, then got himself hurt in a complicated murder situation. Louisa had spent months traveling between Bliss and Cromwell to care for him during his recovery.

I jaywalked across the street and onto the grass, hurrying in his direction.

A small white pickup idled at the curb across the square,

its exhaust visible in the morning air. Based on the truck's position, I couldn't help wondering if the driver was looking at the recently vacated storefront beside it, wondering, as I was, what kind of shop would be there next?

"Mr. Eggers," I called, waving an arm overhead to catch Travis's attention.

"Bonnie?" he asked, recognition lighting his eyes. "Good morning."

"Hi." I stopped before him, my breath puffing out like the truck's exhaust. "I wondered if you heard about what's going on with Louisa."

He nodded somberly. "I have and I hate it," he said. "I'm barely over what happened in Bliss. Now this is happening in her town? It's not right. Definitely not fair. The poor thing's been through so much already." He absently rubbed his head, where a scar from his attack likely ran beneath the hairline.

"I'm sorry," I said, wondering what he'd meant about Louisa already being through so much, but I didn't want to push. "I hate it too," I said instead. "I'd like to help if I can."

He dropped his hand to his side and searched me with his gaze. "You would?" he asked, lowering his voice to a near whisper. "Even over there?"

I nodded. "Yes, sir. I've gotten to know Louisa a bit, and she and Lexi are close. Lexi is my shopkeep. Louisa babysat for her. I care about them both."

"I know Lexi." He rubbed his stubbled chin, glancing past me to my store. "She's a nice girl. I hate to think of you getting involved in another bad situation. Even to help my niece. She wouldn't want you getting hurt either."

"I won't get hurt. I'm just hoping to be another set of eyes and ears for Sheriff Wright. The Cromwell police asked for his help, and he and I are friends, so I thought..." I trailed off, unable to make a case for snooping if Mr. Eggers was determined not to help me. "I was there when they pulled Ben from the lake," I said, changing the subject and drawing him back into the details. "I was shocked to see him in such expensive clothing, considering the lifestyle Louisa has chosen. It's a wonder those two ever made a pair."

Mr. Eggers pursed his lips. "If you ask me, that man was only after one thing from my niece." His frown deepened. "Her chicken."

I blinked.

He grimaced. "Thelma could be a star, but she's a show chicken, not a movie hen. Looking fancy before a set of live-stock judges is one thing, being paraded around in search of commercial and television roles is another. It's not what she or Louisa wanted, and Ben hated that. All he saw when he looked at them were dollar signs."

I nodded solemnly.

"I knew he was no good for her," Mr. Eggers went on. "He moved too fast. Swept Louisa off her feet, injected himself into her community, pretended she was the sun, moon and stars until she was hooked. Then he started asking her to change, expecting her to accommodate him, take his advice. You name it. And he wasn't even any help to her. Louisa thought it was because he wasn't accustomed to farm life, but I think he was lazy. All his constant presence did was add to Louisa's workload, giving her one more person to care for. He'd just walk the lands with her asking questions, while she fed the hens and tended to business. He never helped. It wasn't right."

I absorbed the details, adding them to a growing stack of reasons I didn't like Ben Reid. *Rest his soul.* "Louisa raises Polish hens, but only Thelma is missing," I said, a new line of questions coming to mind. "If all her hens are of equal qual-ity, what made Thelma special? Do you think it's because she was Louisa's personal favorite? Or is there a personality element that makes Thelma a blue-ribbon chicken?" I didn't have the first clue what poultry judges looked for in a speci-men, and I hoped Mr. Eggers might.

He considered the questions a long moment before answering. "You know, I'm not completely certain, having never raised poultry myself. You'd have to ask a judge. Or, if you're really planning a trip to Meadowbrook, you could ask Louisa, or that girl who's always a runner up to Louisa and her hen."

"A runner up?" I asked, feeling a new piece of the puzzle appear on my mat.

He nodded. "I believe her name is Mary."

"Mary Acres?" I asked, recalling the angry brunette with vivid detail.

"That's it," he said. "I hear she's an excellent chicken breeder, but her hens never seem to get the blue."

My mouth fell open. "Mary Acres was also Ben's new girlfriend."

And the name of the woman who'd accused Louisa of his murder.

I was definitely paying her a visit.

CHAPTER SEVEN

I headed back toward my car but changed directions when I saw Liz at What the Dickens drag a sandwich board sign outside the bookstore followed by a rolling cart of books.

As I drew nearer, the message on the sandwich board became clear, and I laughed.

Cold? Buy a book!
You'll still be cold but with a book!

A solid point.

I pulled open the door and stepped inside, warmed instantly by the blowing heater overhead.

"Bonnie!" Liz called, smiling from behind a tall stack of books. "How are you?" She hurried around the table where she'd been making some kind of romantic comedy display. She'd pinned back her light brown hair using golden pins with crystal flowers, and cat-eye glasses perched on her short nose, outlining her bright eyes. In that moment, surrounded by the scent of old books, she reminded me so much of her grandmother, the nostalgia nearly knocked me back to my childhood.

"Hey," I said, shaking the thought aside. "Gigi sent me for the book club book."

"Oh," she said, looking delighted. "I wondered why those copies had appeared on my counter. I thought about trying to put them away, but you know how that goes around here." She rolled her eyes.

I smiled.

Liz often said odd things about the store, which either made her sound a little bizarre or the store a little haunted. I chose not to think too long or hard about the latter.

"Looks like you're getting set up for Valentine's Day in here." I moved toward the table of romance novels where she'd been working. Most with bright, cartoony covers.

She sighed. "Thanks. I'm trying."

I offered her a warm smile, and the stack of books clattered to the floor on the opposite side of the table. I jumped. "Goodness! I am so sorry. I wasn't looking. My purse must've bumped them."

Liz released a labored breath and shot an angry look around the ceiling. "It wasn't you. It's par for the course. Don't bother trying to pick them up. I'll get them in a minute."

I crouched to peek under the table, but there weren't any books on the floor.

She waved a tired hand and lifted the stack of paperbacks near her register. "Are all three copies for you?" she asked.

"I guess so." I fished my wallet from my handbag. "I was on the fence about coming, but Gigi said Sutton is in town and they're both attending. I should probably come too. I don't want to risk missing her while she's here."

Liz rang up the order with a smile. "You didn't think you'd decided, but clearly you had."

I eyeballed the trio of books, then glanced at the display table and the floor beneath. I took a deep breath and reminded myself I had my hands full of unanswered questions already. "I hate that I won't have time to read the novel in time for the meeting."

"Don't worry about it," Liz said, dropping the books into a logoed bag. "Most of the club members come to visit and eat cheese. The book talk is minimal in comparison."

"All right." I smiled. That scenario worked out well for me. I was always down for a good chat and cheese.

Liz gave me the total, then wrinkled her nose. "This must mean your mom isn't coming."

"Probably not. She and Dad are swamped at the farm. This is their busiest time of year, second to Mother's Day," I said.

She nodded. "Makes sense."

My eyes dropped to the bag, and my mind began to pose new questions.

How had the novels gotten to her register? And if I'd decided to come to book club without realizing, how did whoever brought three copies to the register know?

No. I shook my head. *No time. Missing chicken. Murdered man. Worried friend.*

"How's the table coming along?" she asked, reminding me of the special project I'd been working on at home. "I plan to put it right up front when it gets here."

"It's going very well," I said. "I think you're going to love the results."

Liz had asked me to refinish a large round table that belonged to her grandmother. The piece had been a feature in the bookstore since the day it opened, and hundreds of books had sat proudly on top over the years. As a result, the finish had dulled over time, and the wood was chipped and battered at the edges from age and wear. Liz's grandmama

Hazel had cherished the table, handmade by her grandfather. So Liz had requested a revamp of the family heirloom, and I'd obliged. Midnight-blue paint, accented with golden trim and a stenciled mandala pattern at the center. The results were magnificent. I couldn't wait for her to see.

Her expression turned curious, and she tipped her head over one shoulder. "Did it give you any trouble? I've been wondering if things are the same outside the shop as they are in here. Like, do the books go home with people, then give the new owners fits?"

"No," I said, passing her my credit card with a frown. "The table hasn't been any trouble."

"Right." She nodded sheepishly and looked away, concentrating on the credit card.

"I'll ask my dad to bring the table back to you soon. The paint is dry to the touch, but I'd like to see it set for a little longer before it's used for anything. Giving all the coats extra time to harden is always a good idea."

She returned my card and receipt, then passed me the bag. "I can't wait to have it back and choose the perfect books to display." She glared around the shop, as if putting the tomes on notice.

I smiled. "Sounds good. I'll let you know as soon as I can set up the delivery."

"Thank you." She turned away from her register, and the Good Luck Falls calendar on her countertop caught my eye. "Can you believe this year's photos?" she asked, meeting me on my side of the counter and following my gaze to Charles Miller, the Lube Stop owner. "What's it like to date a calendar man?"

"Not bad," I said, feeling a blush rise.

"I'll bet. His photo is my favorite. He made those board shorts look like they should be illegal."

I raised a hand. "Don't tell me. I haven't seen it yet."

She gave me a peculiar look. "The photo?"

My already heated cheeks grew hotter. "I'm waiting to be surprised when I turn the page and it's him."

"Won't you be surprised on the day you turn that page, no matter what? Even if you turn it today?"

"I'm waiting," I said.

Her face screwed up tight. "Why?"

I laughed, unable to think of a decent answer. Miranda had posed a similar question during our last therapy session. Why was I so inclined to delay happiness? To put off certain pleasures and joys? For what? *Why?*

Liz walked me to the door, then snapped her fingers as a gust of cold air rushed in around my ankles and sent a shiver up my spine.

"I almost forgot," she said. "A man was in here looking for you earlier. I didn't recognize him, so I told him I didn't know how to find you. I meant to call right away, but my phone went inconveniently missing." She waved both hands in sudden wild frustration.

"Any ideas who he could've been?" I asked, imagining Eli from Cromwell or even one of the cops in plain clothes. "Can you describe him?"

"He was handsome," she said. "He was only here long enough to ask about you and go. You should check with Gretchen. Maybe he was your soul mate."

Our friend Gretchen owned a holistic store called Golden Matches, where she claimed to identify people's soul mates and predict when and if they would ever meet and how. I loved Gretchen, but I steered clear of love predictions.

"Okay. Thank you," I said again, realizing I'd frozen in the doorway. "See you later."

I moved onto the sidewalk, bag of books in hand, thinking of the man who'd served Louisa papers in my shop. What if Grant was attempting to serve me court papers too?

Could he somehow force me to testify for him?

I scoffed at the thought. He really wouldn't want me to state my thoughts about him while under oath.

I waved to Clyde in my shop window before dropping behind the wheel of my car and shifting into gear. My purse and bag of books rode shotgun.

The drive to my storage unit was short, and on a warmer day, if I hadn't needed to carry a large box back, I might've walked. On this day, however, that was out of the question.

When I'd directed the box of stage props and old-timey clothing to the storage unit, I'd planned to find homes for the unusual things. Perhaps with the high school drama club, local square dancers or scouts.

Now that I knew Louisa and her community existed, I'd offer the items to her first.

I parked my car in the little lot outside the rows of small outbuildings designed to look like individual homes or she-sheds. Each was brightly painted, with a welcome mat and wreath on the door. I used my key to let myself inside, then flipped the light switch. The space was small but tidy, thanks to a long weekend of detailed organization after Christmas. I'd boxed and labeled everything before placing it on the shelves, and I'd used a calendar system for ordering the stacks and piles. I'd never again have to hunt for my spring or fall décor; they were on their respective March and September shelves.

A large decorative rug centered the room, along with an empty table for digging through boxes. Empty boxes had been collapsed, stacked and tucked beneath the shelving units, along with packing tape and scissors. All the supplies necessary to fold a fresh container into existence, should the need arise. Like today.

I located the theater troop's donation and moved it onto the table to explore. Louisa would love the gingham dresses, sun hats and gardening gloves. The old-fashioned aprons would look great on display at the soufflé stand, as would the handful of antique and slightly battered kitchen accessories. I set all those aside while I made a new box from the materials on hand. I transferred Louisa's things into the empty container, then returned the first to the shelf.

I couldn't wait to deliver her things.

The soft scuffing sounds of footfalls wiped the smile from my face as I opened the door.

A long look in both directions confirmed I was alone, but I was certain someone had just rushed away.

I lowered the box in my arms, heart racing as I checked again in each direction. The skin prickled on the back of my neck and gooseflesh coursed over me. I'd been followed before, and maybe it was the past trauma talking, but a voice in my head said *run*!

I locked up quickly, hyper aware of my aloneness.

The cute little storage units seemed suddenly sinister with their cheerful wreaths and welcome mats. Like honey for a trap.

I imagined Ben's killer crouched between them as I dug the keys from my bag, waiting to jump on me as I passed.

So I inhaled deeply, and I ran.

CHAPTER EIGHT

I locked the doors inside my car and stared at the backend of a small white pickup as it rounded the corner out of sight.

Was it the same truck I'd seen on the square earlier? Had it been in the lot with my car a moment before? Had its driver been watching me?

I dug my phone from my purse, telling myself not to be paranoid, while also recalling what Liz had said. Someone she didn't recognize was looking for me.

I pressed speed dial on the last of my frequent contacts. Miranda Ellis, my therapist.

"Hey, Miranda," I said, upon receiving her usual voice-mail. "It's me. Bonnie Balfour."

I started my car and buckled my seatbelt, while repeatedly checking my surroundings. "I was just hoping you might be able to see me a little sooner than our scheduled session," I said as sweetly and sanely as possible. "Got a few things going on that I'd love to talk with you about." I heard the deeply fake ring to my tone. Too precious, and shamefully, exaggeratedly southern. It was the voice I'd used so often in

Atlanta. One I tried never to use now. "You can call or text me back when you have time, if that's possible, or I'll be there at our regular time if you can't bump me up. Thank you so much."

I allowed myself a full body wiggle to shake off the heebie-jeebies as I motored the marshmallow—my white car's nickname—toward Cromwell.

The drive passed in a blur as I worked through the strange happenings of my day. Obviously, I was overthinking and reading too much into the truck and footsteps. No one had threatened me, or paid any attention to me that I could see. And pickup trucks were everywhere in a small town like Bliss.

I'd been through some scary things in the past year, and the residual effects were more apparent at times. Like today. Being present at last night's murder scene had clearly drudged up a lot of barely buried feelings and concerns.

Thankfully, I had Miranda to help me sort it all, and she was good.

My GPS told me to turn onto the next street, and I mentally plugged back in.

I'd read that Cromwell was a mirror image of Bliss in geography and size, but I'd never ventured farther across the boundary than Mason's boat. The people and cultures were practically opposites, according to hearsay, ads and shoppers who'd come from out of town and visited both villages. Bliss had candle shops and home décor. Cromwell had kayak rentals and hiking guides. We had a gazebo on the square. They had a twenty-foot carving of a bear. Bliss was an adorable little town with everything anyone needed to have a beautiful home and happy life. Cromwell was an outdoors-man's paradise. We had the same amount of streams, hills and wildlife, but life in Cromwell focused outside instead of in.

I suddenly wondered if I should've changed into jeans and sneakers or hiking boots so I could better blend in.

Houses soon appeared along the roadside between towns, infrequently at first and mostly made of logs.

A herd of mountain bikers wearing helmet cameras buzzed past. I cringed in my seat, hoping none would come left of center, then I slowed as downtown finally appeared.

The marshmallow and I were immediately dwarfed by oversized trucks with gun racks, bike racks and canoes. I craned my neck to see around the other vehicles as we idled at a red light on the main drag.

A flyer pinned to a nearby telephone pole caught my attention, flapping gently in the winter breeze. The image of a chicken had been centered beneath the word LOST.

I hit my signal and pulled into the next available spot along the curb.

I hopped out at a break in traffic and hustled onto the sidewalk for a closer look at the poster. It took only a moment to confirm the missing chicken was Thelma. Beneath the hen's name and description were instructions to return the bird to Meadowbrook if found. The associated phone number was Louisa's.

A slow look around revealed similar posters attached to every light post and telephone pole in sight, seemingly from here to eternity. Louisa had definitely done her due diligence.

I would've expected nothing less. If Clyde vanished, I wouldn't stop until he was found.

I climbed back into the marshmallow and set my phone into the holder on my dash.

A dark storefront across the street bore the words Baker & Reid Property Investments on its front door. A big CLOSED sign perched in the window. It only took a hot second for my brain to make the connection between the recently deceased, Ben Reid, and the partner's name on the sign.

Was it a coincidence? Did a relative of the victim own the shop and take a day off to grieve, or was Ben a property investor?

I eased back into traffic when the coast was clear and followed my GPS instructions to a pitted dirt path between two fields as far out of town as I thought possible without returning to Bliss. The path led to a distant forest before being swallowed completely.

Several yards away a tree stump large enough to park the marshmallow on had been carved with the words Meadowbrook.

I drove to the tree line, then leaned closer to my steering wheel, attempting to peer into the darkness.

If I drove on, would that make me the equivalent of every numbskull character in every cliched horror novel? Plowing off on their own to see what the strange noise was in the basement.

Honk! Honk!

I leaped and screeched in my seat, squeezing the steering wheel until my knuckles hurt.

Behind me, a box truck bounced gently over the road in my direction.

I toed the gas pedal gingerly, wishing for a place to pull over so the truck could pass, and knowing my little car would probably get stuck if I tried.

Slowly, I rolled forward, my headlights kicking on as the darkness enveloped me.

Here's to hoping I'm not a character in a horror novel.

CHAPTER NINE

I blinked and squinted, adjusting my vision to the shadows caused by profound tree cover. Several yards later, the sun shone down brightly once more.

Small cottages, barns and outbuildings popped onto the landscape, one by one at first, then more often and densely packed. Wooden fences, both pasture-style and picket lined yards and fields. Women in wool coats over dresses tossed feed to penned animals and carried baskets in crooked arms. Men with dark pants and impressive muscles swung axes at wood chunks balanced on tree stumps.

"What on earth," I whispered, barely noticing when the truck behind me pulled off at a mini dairy farm. The image of a cartoon cow became visible as I wound away on the curving road.

"In a quarter mile," the tinny voice of my GPS announced, "your destination will be on your right."

"Thank goodness," I whispered, feeling as if I'd fallen into Wonderland.

Everyone waved merrily as I passed, as if it was completely normal to see a less than ten-year-old Volkswagen in a community where horses and covered wagons seemed the more likely method of transportation.

Music from childhood cartoons and images of animated forest creatures popped into my mind. Bluebirds carrying ribbons, and baby deer standing knock-kneed at the roadside.

It was as if I'd driven into a painting or storybook.

Daffodils and pansies sprouted from window boxes. Tulips and violas grew along the roadside.

I angled into a driveway beside a mailbox marked with Louisa's house number, then took a minute to let the setting sink in.

Several homes had been dark and empty, their curtains gone and yards unkempt. But Louisa's place was an explosion of life and color.

Her little cottage was pale yellow with the kind of high, pointy thatched roof seen in fairytales. A white picket fence outlined her front yard. The wiry brown vines of dormant plants were laced between slats.

I climbed out and made my way onto the tiny porch. A red ladder-back chair with a checkered seat cushion stood near the door, its decorative cross-stitched pillow invited visitors to Sit A Spell.

No doorbell was visible, so I tried the knocker and waited.

Bawk, bawk, bawk.

The repetitive clucks of a chicken turned me around.

A Polish hen with supersized hair hopped onto the porch and puffed its tan and white feathers. I wasn't sure how it could see where it was going.

Another hen hopped onto the porch, followed by two more, and I suddenly wondered if I was being taken captive.

"Excuse me," I said, inching past them before my imagination got the best of me. "Pardon." I hurried off the porch and around the side of the house. Hopefully, if the hens were out, Louisa was as well.

A two-rail wooden pasture fence lined the driveway, presumably dividing her property from the neighbor's. Soon an adorable pale-gray outbuilding came into view. It was designed to look like a little cottage, complete with black-and-white trim, and window boxes with flowers. I was willing to bet it was the upgraded hen house Ben had insisted Louisa buy.

The door to the building was open with a ramp poking into the grass. A white picket fence, like the one in Louisa's front yard, surrounded the hen house.

If this fence was meant to contain the hens, it wasn't working.

"Louisa?" I called over the rhythmic clucking of chickens and distant chopping of wood. "Are you home?"

A muffled sob reached my ears on the wind, and I hurried to the building's open door. "Louisa?"

She sat in a heap on the floorboards, beside two rows of feathered nests. Her blue dress and white apron reminded me of Belle from *Beauty and the Beast*, as did her low pony tail and simple black shoes. A woven shawl lay in the hay behind her, presumably dislodged from her shoulders when she sat down to cry.

"Hey," I said softly. "Are you okay?"

She startled, then blinked. "Bonnie?"

I raised my palms in a show of innocence and smiled. "Surprise."

"What are you doing here?" she asked, wiping swollen red eyes.

"I came to check on you. How are doing?" I lifted the shawl to her shoulders, regretting the dumb question. No one who was doing well would sit alone and sob.

Especially in the cold.

"Ben is dead," she said. "Thelma is missing. Mary thinks I'm a killer. I was humiliated in front of all those people last night when she said so, and word of her accusation has probably spread through the whole town by now. No one will want to buy my soufflés. Everything is bad," she said. "Why is all of this happening?"

"I don't know," I admitted, "but I'm going to help you figure it out. Do you want to go inside and talk where it's warmer?"

I supposed it was rude to invite myself in, but it also wasn't exactly polite to drop by unannounced, so I was already on the wrong side of good manners.

Louisa nodded and let me help her up. She lifted a basket I hadn't noticed from the floor where she'd sat. There was a pile of small white eggs inside, cushioned by a blue-and-white checkered cloth.

"Those are beautiful," I said. "Are they all from these hens?"

She nodded. "Polish hens aren't big layers, but they get the job done and keep everyone I know in quiche."

I smiled, realizing I liked Louisa a little more with every encounter. She was delightful, with a distinct and fun fashion sense. Plus she loved animals and her community. All my favorite qualities in a human.

Louisa led me across her backyard, waving to an older woman with a pair of miniature donkeys. "Hello, Mrs. Pankin," she said.

The woman eyed me cautiously as we approached, a small, pleasant smile on her lips.

"Mrs. Pankin's family helped establish this community," Louisa explained. "She helps me with my donkeys, Jack and Jill."

"You have donkeys?"

"One of the neighbors moved a few months ago and

couldn't take them with them, so I made room here," she said.

Mrs. Pankin waved. "Feeling any better, Louisa?"

"I'm trying," she answered, forcing a tight smile.

"This too shall pass," Mrs. Pankin assured. "It's nice to meet you," she said, moving her attention back to me.

"Bonnie," I said. "Bonnie Balfour."

She nodded, and her silver hair shone in the sunlight. Her skin was tan and loose. Her back a little hunched. I guessed Mrs. Pankin was about my mama's age, but her life had probably been physically harder.

"I'm a bit like a mother to this place," she said. "I do what I can to help folks out."

"She does," Louisa agreed.

"Then you must like Eli," I said, recalling Louisa's suggestion that he was quick to settle disputes.

The older woman's smile widened. "And I'm not the only one."

Louisa blushed furiously as she waved and turned for her back door. "Want some tea? I'll put a kettle on."

The chickens who'd found me on the front porch seemed to have relocated to the back.

Bawk, bawk, bawk.

"No," Louisa said softly. "She hasn't returned, and I know you're worried about her. I am too." She reached into her apron and cast a handful of feed into the grass.

The hens went for it, and Louisa let us inside.

"Never fails," she said. "It works with people too sometimes."

I laughed as I followed her into the warmth.

The inside of her home was small and cramped in a type of cluttered chaos reminiscent of a country craft store. No inch of wall had been left bare. No nook or cranny unused. A cobblestone fireplace rose up between the kitchen and the front room, acting as a partial wall and opening on both sides to better distribute the heat. Paintings, photos and wooden carvings hung in clusters. Tea sets, mixing bowls and canned foods lined shelves.

She pulled a kettle from a rack above a small rolling island and filled it with water from a sink overlooking the side yard. An herb garden grew in pots on the window sill. Bouquets of dried flowers hung upside down from the ceiling, and bundles of greens lay in neat stacks on the counter. "Do you like chamomile?" she asked, setting the pot on the stove.

"I like all tea," I said, helping myself to a green-legged stool beside the island.

She adjusted the gas flame, then took a seat on the stool beside mine. "Sorry I'm kind of a mess right now," she said. "I know bad things happen everywhere, but nothing like this ever happens here. Not in Meadowbrook."

"Technically Ben wasn't from your community. And he was found near the lake, which is on the outskirts of town."

"But I'm from this community. Ben was my boyfriend, at least for a little while, and Thelma is my chicken." Her eyes glossed with new tears, and I immediately felt awful.

"Sorry," I said. "I didn't mean to be insensitive. I'm here to help you get to the bottom of all this, and I think I can."

"How?"

"I'm not sure yet," I admitted, "but I'm willing to try, and these things usually work out for me. Would you mind answering a few questions?"

"Of course. Anything you want to know."

I rubbed my hands down my thighs, preparing to dive in. "Mary said she's Ben's new girlfriend. She's part of this community?"

Louisa's gaze turned curious. "Yes. She lives near the

community garden. You passed her place on your way to mine."

I made a mental note to look more closely at the homes on my way out. "I got the impression last night that you and Mary aren't friends. Were you close before she started dating your ex?"

"No." Louisa looked stricken. "Mary has never liked me. I don't know why."

"Maybe it was because she and her hens never won first place," I suggested, remembering what Mr. Eggers had told me.

"Maybe," Louisa said. "I can't be sure because we've never really talked. Her hens are very nice. I hate that she's never had a chance to win, but Thelma is really something special." Her voice cracked on her pet's name, and she raised her apron to blot her nose.

"Do you think there's any possibility Mary let Thelma loose?" I asked. "Or got into an argument with Ben that ended poorly?"

"Heavens, no," she said automatically, then stilled. She checked the window and door. "Why? Do you?"

"I don't know. These aren't my neighbors and friends. What matters is what you think."

"Right," Louisa said. "Of course."

"What does your gut say?"

She frowned, clearly giving my question serious thought. When her eyes met mine again, she said, "I don't know."

I puffed out a breath. "Any idea who'd want to hurt Ben? Did he mention having problems with anyone? Maybe someone who isn't part of this community?"

"He argued with his business partner a lot. I think that's what brought him to me. He needed an escape."

A disgruntled business partner sounded like a legitimate suspect to me. "I noticed a property-investments office with his last name on the door while I drove through town. Was that his place of business?"

She nodded. "Yep."

"What did Ben and his partner argue about?" I asked.

The kettle sang, and Louisa rose to fix the tea. "They mostly disagreed on which investments to back and how extensively."

"Any specific examples?"

She set two teacups on saucers and filled them both with hot water. Then, she filled two infusers with dried leaves and lowered one into each cup. "The farmcation project was an ongoing debate between them," she said.

"The what?"

Louisa straightened, looking at something in the next room, beyond the fireplace. "I think someone's out front. I'd better go see."

"Wait. What's a farmcation?" I asked, hoping it wasn't what it sounded like.

She delivered our cups to the island but didn't sit. "It's a vacation spent on a working farm."

I frowned. Apparently it was exactly what it sounded like.

"Ben and his partner planned to buy some land in our community and build a lodge for travelers to vacation and experience the cottagecore lifestyle," she said, wringing her hands into her apron. "They thought placing the lodge here would help immerse guests in the full experience. There was going to be a spa and farm-to-fork dining and everything."

A heavy knock on her front door sent Louisa toward the sound. "I'll be right back."

I typed farmcation into a search engine on my phone and marveled when it knew what I was trying to spell. The results confirmed it. A farmcation was a vacation spent experiencing an idealized slice of farm life.

"Huh." I set my phone down as two sets of footfalls returned to the kitchen.

Louisa carried a bouquet of flowers wrapped in paper and tied with a ribbon.

Eli paused awkwardly in the archway between rooms.

"Bonnie, you remember Eli," Louisa said, setting the flowers on the counter and upturning a third cup for tea.

"I do," I said. "Nice to see you again."

He nodded.

"How's your day so far?" I asked Eli, when neither he nor Louisa said another word.

"Not great," he said. "I've been looking for Thelma since dawn."

Louisa turned. "You have?"

"Yeah." He dipped his ridiculously square chin. "I haven't had any luck."

"Well, I appreciate the flowers," she said.

I set my chin on my hand, enjoying their sweet, clueless exchange.

A little voice in my mind chanted *kiss, kiss, kiss, kiss.*

Eli squirmed. "They're not from me," he said sheepishly. "I ran into the delivery man on my way, and I told him I'd bring them the rest of the way."

Louisa's pleasant expression fell. "Oh. Who are they from?"

He shrugged, glancing at me, then at the floor.

She removed a white envelope from the flowers and opened the card.

"Who was it?" Eli and I asked, our voices echoing off one another.

"Ben's partner at the investment firm." Her expression soured. "He says he's sorry for my loss."

Eli grunted.

Louisa poured him a cup of tea and ferried it his way.

He pulled a chair from the corner and lowered himself onto it.

I gave the flowers and note another moment of thought. "Eli, who would you say is the most generally well liked person in the community?"

"Mrs. Pankin," Louisa said. "As one of the founders, she's very well respected."

Eli frowned. "Yeah, but not everyone likes her. She can be persnickety about cell phones and Wi-Fi, which no one wants to give up, and too much chatter about things beyond the community."

Louisa bobbed her head. "She's been here a long time. She really believes in this way of life. She's always saying it would be nice to see the community full again, like it was a few decades ago."

I wasn't sure if that made her a proponent of the farmcation project or an enemy. Getting folks to experience the farmlife from the vantage of a fancy lodge in Meadowbrook could result in more citizens of their fair haven, or maybe having civilians tramping around her beloved land would only frustrate and upset her. I made a mental note to get her thoughts on the matter, but pressed on before I lost the thread I was pulling. "Okay, but is she the most influential?"

Eli's eyes turned to Louisa. "No."

Louisa looked from Eli to me, then back. "You could be right, but if you are, I wouldn't know who is," she said. "Maybe you?"

He barked a disbelieving laugh. "Definitely not me. I rub too many people the wrong way, and I'm not as social as the rest of you." He turned his handsome hazel gaze on me. "Louisa is the one folks look to. They like and trust her. She's the moral compass and exemplifies everything this community was based on."

I made a mental note of the sexy lumberjack before me,

who'd just used the words *persnickety* and *exemplifies* in a matter of minutes. Who was this guy? Where was he from?

Louisa frowned. "Bonnie?"

"Sorry," I said, dragging my thoughts back on track. "So, if a property-investments company wanted to be accepted by your closely tied community, earning Louisa's favor would be a smart move?"

"Definitely," Eli said.

Then the new question was, did Ben Reid think so too? Was that why he'd initially pursued Louisa? Her uncle had thought he'd moved fast. Maybe there was a less-than-romantic reason for it.

"Knock knock," Mrs. Pankin said, letting herself in through the back door with a pie. "I brought a little something sweet to go with our tea."

"Thank you." Louisa said. "That's so kind."

I smiled at the newcomer, grateful for a chance to speak with her soon, and I turned back to Eli. "Did the people who left their donkeys with Louisa leave Meadowbrook because of the farmcation?"

He rubbed a giant hand over his stubbled cheek. "It's possible. Not everyone is in favor of it, but there's also not much we can do to stop it. We don't own the whole forest."

Mrs. Pankin set her pie on the counter and poured herself some tea.

I waited for eye contact with the older woman, eager to ask her thoughts on the farmcation.

Someone rapped at the door, pulling our attention to the front of the home again.

Louisa sighed. "I'm sorry. Excuse me."

"Is it always this busy here?" I asked. "Or is this because of Ben's death?"

"Both," Eli said. "Folks are always coming and going, but I

suppose there wouldn't have been a flower delivery, and you wouldn't be here if not for the murder."

"Touché," I said, finally sipping my now tepid tea.

Louisa reappeared a moment later with a uniformed cop.

Mrs. Pankin and I stilled.

Eli stood.

The female officer scanned the room with interest, then fixed her attention on the only man in the kitchen. "Eli, I've been told you threatened Ben Reid with your ax last week, and I'm going to need you to come with me to the station so we can discuss that."

My jaw dropped, as did Louisa's and Mrs. Pankin's.

Eli dipped his chin without objection and let her lead him back through the little cottage.

"Eli?" Louisa said.

He offered an apologetic look over his shoulder. "You knew I didn't like him," he said. "He was trouble."

"Stop talking!" I yelled, earning a dirty look from the cop.

I pressed my lips together and shrugged.

We followed in single file, spilling onto the porch in silence while the officer stuffed Eli into a cruiser waiting beside the marshmallow in Louisa's driveway.

The officer looked comically small as she rose onto her toes to guide his head into the back seat before closing the door.

Across the street, Mary Acres sneered in unmistakable delight.

CHAPTER TEN

I waited at my shop door for Mason to arrive the next morning. He'd been too busy to stop by last night, and he hadn't said why. The implication had been that he was caught up in the Cromwell murder investigation, but the pinch in my gut said it was something more, and I wasn't sure how to ask.

"Morning," he said, stepping inside with two disposable cups. A curl of steam rose from the plastic lid on each. "I stopped at a coffee place in Cromwell on my way in. I picked you up a latte."

"Thanks," I said, accepting the peace offering for what it was.

Mason wore dark jeans and black boots today. His black leather coat was unzipped and lined in wool.

Beyond the glass door at his back, a small white pickup idled at the curb across the square.

"Any idea who bought the empty shop space over there?" I asked, dragging my eyes back to Mason.

"No. Why?"

"I'm not sure," I said. "I see a white pickup parked outside it a lot, and I've been noticing the same truck around town these last couple of days. It's probably nothing. I'll have to see if Cami's heard anything about a buyer."

My lifelong best friend, Cami, was the chairwoman of a campaign to bring tourists and locals downtown again, and she worked hard to make shopping at the square fun for everyone. She'd likely know if anyone had shown interest in the space or made the purchase.

Mason turned to follow my gaze.

"Have you heard anything new about the Cromwell case?" I asked. "Any news on Thelma?"

"None," Mason said, returning his attention to me and bending to rest his elbows on my counter. "But it's still possible she's just lost. I read up on missing chickens, and apparently it's not so uncommon for a pampered and protected pet like Thelma to wander off, especially if she was frightened."

My heart melted a little. "You read up on missing chickens?"

He gave me a bland look. "Yes, and it turns out those free-range chicken owners are smart to let their flock wander. Free-range birds learn their way around and don't tend to stray very far. A bird like Thelma, though, who isn't used to wandering, could've gotten spooked and fled, then became disoriented and confused by unfamiliar surroundings. Chances are she's hunkered down somewhere and will turn up."

I grinned. "Good to know. How about the murder? Any leads on who'd want to kill Ben Reid?"

"No."

I offered a bland look. "You answered that one a little fast."

He didn't comment.

"Do you know if Cromwell PD released Eli?"

Mason shook his head. "Not yet as far as I'm aware."

I made a crazy face. "What are they doing? They can't just keep him. Has he even been charged with anything?"

Mason smirked. "I hate to break it to you, but they have every right to hold him up to seventy-two hours while they build a case."

"Seriously?"

He nodded. "Yep."

"Oh." I groaned. "That's dumb."

I needed to watch more true-crime and detective shows or read books about police procedures. The amount of things I didn't know on the subject of law enforcement protocols and procedures was ridiculous and frustrating.

Mason smiled. "Eli's going to be fine. He's tough and likely innocent. He'll be free soon. Until then, I'm doing everything I can to speed this investigation along."

"Thank you. Louisa's beside herself. First losing Thelma, now, Eli. I'm not sure who she turns to for comfort when they're both gone."

"She and Eli are close?" Mason asked.

"I think she's in love with him. She doesn't think he's noticed her in that way, but he has. I saw it with my own eyes. Not to mention, he wouldn't be leading the charge to find her chicken if he wasn't pining over her. And he admires her. He thinks she's the most influential person in their community."

"Isn't he a little old for her?" Mason asked.

"Not really. Lexi's nineteen, so Louisa must be in her mid-twenties. She guessed him at thirty." I waved a dismissive hand. "I'm going to plan their wedding."

Mason rolled his eyes. "Will you let them know first or just trick them into showing up at the same place and time, then start reading their vows?"

"You think I'm pushy," I said, smiling. "But I just know things."

"Uh huh," he said, smiling back as he took another drink of coffee.

"I do," I insisted. "For example, I know the people in Louisa's community rely on one another. They're a team and a family. And they respect Louisa. Ben Reid, on the other hand, was a businessman looking to disrupt their lives with a farmcation establishment, including a spa and fine dining, luring in out of towners. He was the kind of man who'd sue a woman over custody of her beloved chicken. There's no way a pushy, pretentious person like that could win any friends in Meadowbrook on his own, and he knew it. So he hitched his wagon to Louisa."

Mason sucked his teeth. "You think he used her to gain a footing for his business venture."

I nodded. "Yep. Then there's Mary, the perpetual runner up on the chicken-breeder circuit. She accused Louisa of killing Ben the night before last, and I'm sure she had a hand in getting Eli hauled in yesterday. I'm not sure what her beef is with Eli, but removing Thelma from the next poultry judging practically guarantees her hen a blue ribbon." I thought things through another moment and added, "Louisa said Mary's never liked her, so maybe causing Eli trouble was more about upsetting Louisa than Eli. Assuming she has two eyes, she surely knows what I know about those two."

Mason's bored expression turned sour. "That they're getting married."

I nodded slowly.

He sighed and tapped his nearly empty cup on the counter. "I had similar thoughts about Ben's interest in Louisa, but I didn't know about the runner-up chickens."

I beamed, then filled him in on everything Mr. Eggers told me and finished my coffee while Mason processed the new information.

"I still want to talk to Mrs. Pankin," I said. "She's the community matriarch, and I'm guessing she has some notable insights on all this."

"Why does it sound like you're building a case?" Mason asked.

I raised an upturned palm and donned my best *beats-me* expression.

The etched glass door between my shop and Gigi's swung open, and Gigi poked her head inside. "I thought I heard a man's voice in here. Just what I need." She vanished back into her bakery.

Mason shot me a concerned glance. "You think she needs me to open a jar or apprehend a burglar?"

"Could be anything," I said. "With Gigi, the suspense is half the fun."

She returned a moment later with a bright smile and small platter of sweets. Her hair was wrangled beneath a hairnet, and she wore a logoed Oh My Goodies apron over her red turtleneck and elastic-waisted jeans. White orthopedic sneakers carried her in our direction at double-time. "I need a taste tester."

I smiled at her enthusiasm. "You need a man to taste these?"

Mason's eyes widened at the assortment of sweets on the tray.

"I need a varied audience," she said. "Everyone who stopped to see me today was female, and I made a big change to my recipes."

He lifted a chocolate cake sample to his lips first, then hummed in pleasure as he set it on his tongue.

"What's the change?" I asked, dragging my eyes from Mason's thoroughly satisfied face.

"I made all of these with Louisa's eggs," Gigi said. "They're amazing. At first I was just curious to see how much of a flavor difference they'd make, because I might be able to buy from her sometimes, if that would help her."

Mason moaned beside me, and I plucked the material of my shirt near the collar, attempting to circulate the suddenly warm air.

"...superior in every way," Gigi continued. "I couldn't believe it. I'm not sure I ever want to use any other eggs again if I don't have to."

I selected a sample of what looked like almond pound cake, curiosity piqued. The flavors melted over my tastebuds. Rich and sweet. The texture was silk on my tongue. "Glory," I whispered.

"I know!" Gigi exclaimed, rocking onto her toes. "I can't even imagine what her soufflés must taste like. I bet they're addictive. I want one right now."

I laughed.

Mason's phone rang, and he gave it a frown. "I've got to go. These are amazing, Gigi. Thank you." He selected a strawberry tart, then sucked the icing from his thumb. His eyelids fluttered a little.

"We weren't finished talking," I said. "Here. Take these with you for later." I hurried to my handbag and retrieved a stack of blank thank-you cards. "For your casserole givers."

He licked a smidge of frosting from the tip of his thumb, and I saw stars. "Thanks." He tucked the cards into the interior pocket of his coat, then winked when he looked at me once more. "You're going to have to help me with those."

"I will," I promised, knowing I would forever envy that little dollop of buttercream.

Mason stacked a few more of Gigi's samples on his massive palm for the road. "I'm sorry to run out, but we'll talk tonight, okay?" He dropped a kiss on my cheek, and I sighed.

"Okay."

"Thanks again, Gigi. These are all phenomenal." He spun away, barely glancing up as he sidestepped a man on his way through the door. He was already on the sidewalk, passing my window, then out of view before I found my voice to greet the newcomer.

My skin crawled and my joints locked as our eyes met.

"Hello, Grant."

CHAPTER ELEVEN

My ex-husband strode inside like he owned the place. The only way he went anywhere. He'd spiked his dark hair and chosen the wayfarer style of designer glasses he thought made him look younger and carefree. Even his sneakers and metallic-gray ski coat were part of the cool, casual façade. Quite an elaborate act. I was too stunned to guess its purpose.

But I couldn't help wondering if he'd traded his Jaguar for a white pickup.

It took a moment for me to realize my mouth had gone dry, and my chest burned from lack of oxygen. My next inhalation came in a thin, searing sip.

"There you are," he said, removing his sunglasses from his face and hanging them from scooped neckline of his shirt beneath the coat. "Finally. I've been asking around about you for days. I guess you didn't make the big splash you'd hoped by coming home. Most folks didn't even know who I meant when I said your name." He made a derisive, snorting sound and shook his head, then smiled. "Not to worry. I'm sure you'll make a place for yourself eventually. It takes time to build a reputation someplace new. Anyway, now that I found you, I'm hoping we can talk."

He scanned the store, clearly unimpressed. "Oh, hey, Gigi," he said, as if he'd just noticed her. "Long time no see."

"Lucky me," she said flatly. "What are you doing here?"

His smile grew, showcasing a mouth full of expensive caps. "That's a funny story. I actually have some business with my wife," he said, swinging his gaze back to meet mine. "I tried talking to her by phone, but she threatened to call the cops." His tone turned hard, and I squirmed beneath it. "You said no more phone calls, so here I am."

I felt my shoulders curve under the weight of his stare, and it became more difficult to breathe or swallow. I knew the smile on his face for what it was. Predatory.

He'd come to threaten me. To insist I write the letter he'd asked for. To do what he said or he'd make me pay in some way.

Gigi moved to my side, and I focused on her strength because mine had fled at the sight of him. "Blissers don't make a habit of telling strange men where to find women in our town," she snapped. "Those folks you spoke to lied to your face, because they were protecting her. People know exactly who Bonnie is."

"You guys call yourselves blisters?" Grant laughed. "Weird. I don't get it, but to each his own, right?" He chuckled, amused at our small-town hijinks. "I guess it's probably good to have a sense of humor here."

My muscles tensed at the condescending way he spoke to my grandmama, and my mouth finally opened. "I didn't just tell you not to call," I said, voice weak. "I told you to leave me alone. And I am not your wife anymore." The words rattled as I spoke them, lacking the punch I'd hoped for.

Grant stuck out his bottom lip. "Is that what this is about? Your feelings are hurt because I finally pulled the plug on our miserable marriage? I was patient with you far longer than anyone else would've been. You'd been trying to drag me to counseling for years before I finally said enough. No one else would've stuck around that long. Obviously you were never going to be happy. Eventually I had to stop letting you put that on me." He shook his head disdainfully, truly put out by the burden I'd been.

"That's enough," I growled, feeling the rage growing inside me. And embracing it.

He cocked a brow, interested, but not happy. No one spoke to him that way. Ever. "Let me take you out to dinner," he said. "We can talk this out."

"No."

"I'll wait," he said, raising his palms in a truce. "We can go as soon as you finish shopping." He gave the store another distasteful look. "We can even bring Gigi if you'd like."

"I'm not shopping. This is my store. And I already have dinner plans."

Grant's expression tightened a moment before fading into the veil of civility he typically wore in public. "Well, at least you've put my money to terrible use," he said dryly. "And I suppose your plans are with that sullen-looking fellow who passed me on his way out. Did he even say goodbye?"

I bit my tongue and glared, knowing anything I said would be twisted and used against me later.

"Didn't take you long to move on, huh, Bon Bon?"

"Please. Leave," I said. "I don't want to eat dinner with you. I don't want to see you. Go home. Or I will get a restraining order."

Grant's pretense of being anything other than awful crumbled with his next sneer. "You don't tell me what to do," he seethed.

Gigi unearthed her cell phone. "That's it. I'm calling the sheriff."

The door opened behind Grant, and a group of shoppers came inside. They paused to look at the situation. The tension on our faces had to be evident and surely charging the air around us.

"Hello, Bonnie," one of the women said. "How you doing, sweetie?"

"Good," I lied, forcing a smile for her benefit, though I only barely recognized her.

"Gigi," she said. "How are you?"

Another woman from the group stepped between Grant and I, giving him her back. "You know that dress you altered for my granddaughter's wedding was the talk of the night. I almost felt bad for the bride."

"I'm so glad you liked it," I said on autopilot. The words were hollow, and I hated that I couldn't muster an appropriate amount of excitement. Or recall the event she spoke of.

A third woman joined her, smiled warmly and forming a small wall between us and our unwanted guest. "You look just beautiful today," she said. "What I wouldn't give for your fashion sense and style. Don't even get me started on that perfect skin and gorgeous hair."

"Thank you."

Then, as if this strange, unexpected behavior was normal, or a routine they'd performed before, the women turned their bright southern smiles on Grant.

It was harder to see him now, but I imagined his face reddening as he fought the urge to lash out, unable to act on the desire for fear of showing his true colors.

I was the only one he let see that side of him.

Now, he had an audience.

"Are you lost?" the oldest of the woman asked. She raised

oversized glasses from a chain around her neck and slid them onto her nose. "I don't think this is the store you were looking for. Maybe try another. Perhaps in the town you came from."

My jaw nearly unhinged as I waited for Grant's head to explode.

Gigi plucked an earring from her lobe and raised her phone to her ear. "Hello, is this the sheriff's department?"

Grant spun and planted his palms against my door with a jarring thud.

The door smacked against the wall outside as he stormed away.

And I had just made three new friends for life.

CHAPTER TWELVE

My phone rang at seven, and Mason's face appeared on the screen. I smiled as I answered, despite the earlier run-in with Grant. Because in a few minutes, I would be with my best friend, eating good food and telling him all about the bully who turned red when he realized he couldn't bully me anymore. And the way a group of women I'd barely recognized, but would now forever adore, had sensed the trauma and become a unified light that sent the cockroach running.

And the way watching him walk away had buoyed me.

My therapist was going to love this story.

"Hello," I said, flipping off the store lights and pulling my purse onto one shoulder.

Clyde looked up at me from his place inside the cat carrier, impatient for his dinner. Thelma's feather lay with him, trapped beneath one paw.

"Hey," Mason said. "I really hate to do this, but can I get a rain check on dinner? Something's come up, and it's probably best if I deal with it sooner rather than later."

I paused to slump against the counter. This wasn't the

victorious celebratory evening I'd wanted. "I guess so. What's going on?"

"Errr…" Mason made a soft, deliberating sound.

"I hope we aren't doing secrets again," I said. "Because I've kind of enjoyed being transparent with one another."

The ability to tell him anything and everything lately had been freeing. Empowering. And I'd loved it. Being trusted with his secrets in return was even better. He was the only person I didn't censor myself with in some way. I talked to my folks, Cami and Gigi about most things, but I'd always avoided telling them things that might make them worry. With Mason, I didn't have to do that. We'd decided to be straight with one another about everything, which was terrifying and occasionally pretty embarrassing, but once the words were out, I was always lighter and deeply thankful. I wasn't ready to give that up.

"Work," he said finally. "Just some things that've been pushed aside all day while I dealt with the Cromwell murder."

"Can't a deputy do whatever it is?" I asked, knowing Bliss had a fully staffed, fully capable force at his disposal.

"Sheriff stuff," he said. "I need to do it."

I deflated and debated pushing this issue, but knew I wouldn't change his mind. My screaming intuition said he wouldn't cancel last-minute without good reason, and I worried the reason wasn't really sheriff stuff, like he'd said. In fact, for the last few months, anytime he behaved the slightest bit squirrely, I feared his past had come back to haunt him.

As a homicide detective in Cleveland, Mason had gone undercover, working in conjunction with the local FBI, to bust up a crime ring they called The Investors. He'd become emotionally tangled with a woman who'd given her life to protect his secret when she found out, and he'd been forced to let that tragedy lay. He carried guilt and shame by the truckload, and moving here was supposed to help him find perspective and peace. He was working on it, but I wasn't sure people ever truly got over the kind of thing he'd been through.

"I am sorry," he said. "How was your day after I left?"

I barked a humorless laugh. "Oh boy," I said, smiling at the reminder. "I wanted to tell you over dinner. Are you sitting down?"

Mason was silent for a long beat. "What happened?"

I released a steadying breath, then spilled the tale.

Strangely, as I voiced the story I'd played in my head a dozen times, my throat tightened and my eyes began to sting.

"Grant's in town?" Mason growled. "Now?"

I nodded, voice suddenly failing. "Mm hmm."

"And he came to your store to badger you into saying he wasn't a total creep?"

I swallowed several times, attempting to clear the lump swelling in my throat. "I don't think he cares if I say he was a terrible husband," I croaked. "I think I'm supposed to say he doesn't deserve jail time for hiding all our money offshore and lying about it." I tried to inhale again, but the breath was shuddered, and I felt the twinges of a building panic attack.

"Bonnie," Mason said softly. "You're okay."

"Kay," I echoed, letting him be the touchstone that kept me anchored, even if I couldn't actually touch him.

Panic attacks had become a fun little thing my mind and body did these days, usually when I least expected it. Mason and Miranda were helping me learn to navigate the experiences so I could eventually cut the attacks off before they took over.

"This is a trauma response," he said, apparently hearing the change in my tone or breathing. "You don't have to be afraid of it. Being afraid because you feel afraid makes it worse, and you don't have to be afraid now, because I'm with you, and I can be there in a few minutes if you need me. But you are safe. Hear me?"

I nodded, though my eyes had somehow closed and I knew he couldn't see me. "Kay," I repeated.

"You lived in a low-key, simmering state of emotional distress for years, and Grant's a trigger," Mason continued, talking me through the panic, as he had since the attacks had recently begun, a full year after I'd left the awful situation. Just when I'd thought I was healed. "You reacted normally to seeing him again, here in your world. A safe place you've built for yourself with time, effort and love. Your feelings are justified."

I slowly forced the breath from my lungs and refilled them with a deep, fresh inhalation. "Thank you."

"You want me to assign someone to follow him around?" Mason asked. "Maybe dole out a bunch of citations? Speeding ticket, parking ticket, something from the archive? Did you know this town has a law saying a man can be fined for not walking nearest the curb if a lady is present on the sidewalk with him? He doesn't even have to know the woman. Imagine how many fines he could rack up without knowing what's happening."

I laughed, and a measure of the weight on my chest lifted.

It was strange to talk to Mason about Grant, but I deeply appreciated his kindness on the matter. Thankfully, he didn't seem to care about my past. He listened but never judged. Another aspect of him I'd come to count on.

Amidst our fantastic banter, and occasional butting of heads, Mason had become my happy place and landing pad.

"Feeling any better?" he asked.

"Yeah," I answered honestly, no longer caring that he wasn't available for dinner. "Thank you."

"Anytime. And the offer stands. What's the point of being sheriff if I can't run folks out of town from time to time?"

I laughed again. "Always so power hungry."

I grabbed my car keys, then hefted Clyde's carrier, smiling more brightly. "You can stop by my place later, you know. If you want. I might have to eat alone, but I'd love to share dessert."

The sound of squealing tires raised my attention to the front door. My brain scrambled to make sense of the sight beyond.

Bang! Bang! Bang!

Three projectiles crashed into the glass, and I screamed, dropping to the floor.

I crawled behind my counter, dragging Clyde's carrier in one hand, covering my head with the other.

My cell phone skittered across the floor.

My shop window rattled but didn't break.

And then there was silence.

I peeked a moment later, reaching for my phone and surveying the damage. My shop door and large display window were smeared with broken eggs.

Mason arrived only minutes later, face red and body tense. He pulled me into a hug when I unlocked the door for him, then he walked me to a chair and got me a bottle of water from my mini fridge.

He trembled with what seemed to be a mix of fear and rage.

"Are you okay?" I asked, gulping the water.

He nodded and scraped one hand through his messy hair. "I heard you scream and thought Grant had come back to hurt you."

I set the half-empty bottle on the floor at my feet with trembling hands. "He wouldn't. He's never been violent."

Mason narrowed his eyes, as if he had more to say on the subject, but didn't. "You okay to sit here while I take some photos and gather evidence?"

"Yeah."

He turned for the door, and I rose to follow.

He frowned. "I guess you're feeling like yourself again."

"Maybe." I hadn't fully recovered from the shock, and my body wanted to remain in the chair, but curiosity had won out.

Curiosity always won out.

I stared at the egg yolks and bits of cracked shell still clinging to the glass. "So, this is definitely about the chicken," I said.

"Or Louisa Eggers," he said, snapping photos of the mess from every angle, then the street where the vehicle I'd heard spinning its tires had launched the messy little vessels.

"I told you about the white pickup earlier," I said. "It sits outside the empty storefront, but I also saw it, or one like it, on the street near my storage unit only moments after hearing hurried footfalls outside. I didn't see the vehicle these were thrown from, but I can't help wondering if it was the white truck."

Mason set his hands on his waist, looking both concerned and exhausted. "Tell me this again, with details."

I repeated the story, including the minimal details I could come up with, then waited.

"All right," he said. "Give me ten minutes to clean this up, and I'll follow you home."

I got a bucket of warm soapy water ready while he finished with the crime scene, then we washed my window together, and he walked Clyde and me to our car.

"I don't suppose there's any way I can convince you to

leave this Cromwell thing alone?" he asked. "The missing hen. The murder. All of that?"

I shook my head. "I'm too worried about Louisa. She lives alone, and someone is targeting her. First someone stole her chicken," I said, pausing for a minute so he could let that sink in. I was certain Thelma hadn't simply run off and gotten lost like he'd suggested. The timing was too coincidental and in alignment with Ben's death. "Someone killed her ex-boyfriend. Mary accused her of murder. And now the cops put Louisa's protector in jail."

"Eli isn't in jail," Mason said, helping me into my car.

"Well, he isn't with Louisa either. He's detained and she's alone, so I will absolutely be going back to check on her and trying to help however I can."

Mason rested one arm on the roof of my car and the other on my open door. Then he hung his head closer to mine. "I'll see what I can do to spring Eli tomorrow."

"Tomorrow?" I asked.

He closed my door with a labored sigh.

I powered the window down. Letting him know I was waiting on an answer.

"Not tonight?" I asked.

"No. Tonight I'm going home with my girlfriend." He leveled me with a heated stare, and my gaze fell to his lips.

"Yeah?"

"She had a rough day, and she needs me," he said. "Which is what I should've said as soon as you told me your ex-husband was in town. I'm sorry about that."

Warmth spread through my heart and out to my limbs as he crossed the street to his Jeep and climbed inside. If this was what relationships were supposed to be, I could certainly understand the hype.

CHAPTER THIRTEEN

My therapist, Miranda Ellis, worked in a small downtown apartment over an ice cream shop specializing in real-dairy frozen treats. The shop wasn't on the square, but it wasn't far, and the revitalization Cami had worked so diligently on had spread to reach Udder Delights as well.

I drove to my appointment when Lexi arrived to watch the shop. Miranda's message of an available time slot arrived early this morning, while I was in the shower, and I'd quickly left a response voicemail accepting the appointment.

It was strange to know a therapist existed in Bliss. Small towns were usually such gossip traps, and knowing who was seeing a counselor and guessing why could've easily become a top-tier party game. But Miranda was a ninja of sorts. She'd impressed me from the start, after my general physician gave me her number when I saw him about my panic attacks. Miranda was a level-one ghost outside our times together, and I had no idea how she stayed in business when my car was always the only one in the lot. I didn't even know how she got there.

I never saw another client coming or going. Never heard anyone mention her by name or practice. She had no online presence. I'd checked. Thoroughly. And her office space was too small to live in, with only a half bath. I'd checked that out too on my first visit.

I hurried to the rear door and let myself inside, taking a moment to shiver away the winter air and inhale the sweet scents of vanilla and warm waffle cones that seemed to leak through the walls from Udder Delights.

Noises from the ice cream shop followed the delectable scents as I climbed the interior steps to Miranda's office. Muffled voices and laughter. The clatter of bowls on countertops and spraying of water into a sink.

I smiled as I reached the small square landing. A woven rug covered the floor, and a wrought iron stand pressed against the wall. She'd lined a row of potted succulents on top, along with a stack of classic novels and a decorative lamp.

It was all very lovely and welcoming.

Through the white door, simply adorned with a grapevine wreath and wooden Welcome sign, was a small spa-like waiting area. I took a seat in my usual spot among a variety of attractive options and set my purse on my lap. The coffee table before me held an array of magazines and a scented candle that made me think of days at the seaside. A refreshments table stood beneath a window, covered by a white eyelet curtain. Decaf coffee, herbal tea and water were available. No caffeine. No sugar.

Nothing that might get the clients all jazzed up.

The doorway along the wall across from the front window led to the half bath, and if there was ever a kitchen or kitchenette on this floor, it was nowhere to be found. At least without more snooping than I'd previously done.

I stared at the closed door opposite my seat and wondered.

Had she heard me arrive? Was there a camera to watch the waiting area? Was she watching me now?

The door opened, and I flinched as Miranda stepped into the threshold. A warm smile graced her lips. "Bonnie. It's so nice to see you. Come in."

Miranda was probably in her fifties. She was tall and thin, willowy like a dancer, and she wore a lot of muted blues and grays. Her blond hair was streaked with gray and cut into a nice, sensible bob that dusted her shoulders. Today her pale-blue dress reached her ankles, and a long cream cardigan hung to her knees. She looked fancy, but cuddly, in a way I could never pull off.

I'd worn gray dress pants and a red blouse with pearls.

I moved into her office and Miranda shut the door.

There were two windows in this room, one facing the street and another facing the space between buildings, both had eyelet curtains. She'd painted the walls a milky white that held the faintest hint of blue. There was a desk on one wall. A love seat in front of one window, a side table with a tissue box, and the chair where she sat cross-legged, a notebook on her lap.

"You look lovely today," she said, her delightful British accent enchanting me immediately, as usual. "Bright-eyed and bushy-tailed, I think the saying is. How are things going?"

I was bright-eyed from the adrenaline constantly coursing through my veins since the discovery of another dead body, and I told her so. Then I told her everything else in a long bluster until I sagged in relief to be rid of it all.

"Well," she said, her voice as calm and kind as always. "That certainly is a lot. Isn't it?"

I stared. Was it? I supposed it was, but it also didn't feel like too much.

Did it?

"It's a lot for one person to carry," she continued, clarifying. "You've taken things like this in stride recently, and I'm afraid you're starting to think all of this is just run-of-the-mill life experiences, but they're not."

I waited. Processing.

"The experiences you've been having are extraordinary, and I don't mean that in a better than ordinary way. I mean these are heavy and burdensome things you're going through. When you try to think of them as regular traumas, like excessive traffic or a water leak at your home, you deceive yourself into thinking you should be able to manage them. Most people weren't made to manage this sort of stress. Finding dead bodies is a horrible thing. Thinking about murderers can be scary. Being threatened, stalked, kidnapped. These are all uncommon and incredibly traumatic."

My head began to nod. "They are." And she was right. I did think of them as part of my life now. The same as running my shop and remodeling my home.

"Right," she said. "And here you are again. In the middle of something eerily similar. Now, what are we going to do about that?"

I nodded some more. No wonder I was so on edge all the time. I really needed to help Louisa find Thelma.

"You want to get involved," she said. "But it's not really working out for you, is it?"

I frowned, having missed something. "What?"

She set her glasses on her nose and looked at her notebook. "You've been home a little more than a year now. You're here to heal after what amounts to a near-lifetime of emotional abuse." She looked up at me. "You had nineteen happy years being a kid. Followed by nineteen traumatic years with your ex-husband. And only a bit more than one year here, recuperating."

Tension gripped my chest at the mention of my ex. "Yes."

"So, you come home to heal and challenge yourself," she said gently, a caring expression on her pretty face. "You opened a lovely shop and became a small-business owner. Pretty amazing, isn't it?"

I smiled. "It was hard."

"Yes, but you can do hard things. You proved that to yourself."

"I did."

"Then, what happened when that was settled?" she asked.

My brows furrowed. "What do you mean?"

She leaned forward, resting thin arms on her closed notebook. "When things got a little easier, because your shop was up and running. What happened next?"

I pursed my lips, unsure where she was going with this. "I don't know."

Miranda gave me a minute to think, then carried on. "You had a new trauma. You found the body of a woman in town."

"Right," I said. "Mrs. Abbott-Harrington. It was awful."

"I imagine it was," she agreed. "And you felt accused."

"I was accused," I said.

"So, you got involved in the murder investigation."

"Yes."

"And you know how that went," she said. "Very scary. Frustrating. Dangerous. Until it was solved, and things became easy again."

I nodded. "That's right."

Miranda offered a sad smile. "Then you repeated that cycle at your first opportunity. Why is that, do you think?"

"Uhm." I had no idea, so I waited for her to tell me.

"Then you did it a third time," she said. "And now you're doing it again. Does it feel like a pattern to you?"

I shook my head. "I don't think so."

"Hmm." She straightened and tucked the stem of her glasses between her teeth. "Patterns of behavior sometimes suggest we're looking for something, chasing it even. Any idea what you might be seeking?"

I crossed, then uncrossed my legs, moving my purse to the floor, then back to my lap again, unable to answer.

"I sense you pulling away, so let's put a pin in this and talk about something else. Tell me what's on your mind right now," Miranda said.

I told her about the white truck and the possibility I was being followed. Then I rambled a bit about Grant, and how uneasy having him in my new space made me. Then, I confessed my fears about Mason possibly digging into the crime ring that had caused him so much pain. But I referred to Mason as Cliff, because it was a small town, after all, and I didn't know anyone named Cliff. I referred to the crime ring as some generic trouble from his past.

Opening up to Miranda was hard enough when I was the subject. I wasn't ready to bare Mason's secrets to her as well.

"And the panic attacks are coming more often?" she asked.

"Yes, but they're more manageable now that I know what they are and that they will pass."

"Good." She formed a small encouraging smile with her lips. "Do you think you could work through them without Cliff's assistance?" she asked. "Or has he become necessary to your balance?"

"I can do it without him," I said. "I have."

"Good. And how are things progressing with the new relationship?"

"Slowly," I said.

"Kissing?" she asked. "Physical comfort?"

"Yes."

She tented her brows. "Sex?"

My face burned with unnecessary embarrassment. I gripped my pearls, unable to answer something so private. Every fiber of my upbringing vanquished the answer on my tongue.

"It's not so crazy, is it?" she asked, probably noticing my red-hot face and making her own conclusion. "He's important to you. You trust him, and you care for him. People have been known to engage in that sort of intimacy for much less."

I pressed my lips together and fought the urge to crawl under the sofa. I'd only ever been with Grant in the way she described, and I'd been young and fit then. Exposing a forty-year-old body, with significantly more weight and distinctly less muscle tone, to anyone new was the epitome of terrifying.

Miranda tipped her head and lifted one palm slightly. "All right. No reason to press any hot buttons when there are so many other things to explore."

"Thank you."

"So," she said. "Circling back to your need to interject yourself into murder investigations."

I slouched. She always brought our sessions back to this, and we never sorted it out before my time was up. "I don't need to," I clarified. "I just hate unanswered questions, and I like to help."

"You've said that," she said, opening her book once more. "But it's a vicious cycle, isn't it? When you go after answers to these sorts of questions and help people in these sorts of situations. The danger and fear. The stalking and attacks. Do you have reason to suspect the sheriff's department won't be able to complete the job on their own?"

"No. It's not that. It's just that I..." I shut my mouth, having nowhere to go.

She waited.

I stared. Stumped.

Miranda shifted. "So, I think we really need to work on unpacking the reasons for this particular compulsion. Then we can deal with those one by one. Do you have any guesses?"

"I just want to help," I said. "And I like to know what really happened."

"You could've gotten a private investigator's license and opened one of those offices, or become a law-enforcement officer," she said. "But you opened a second-chance shop."

"I like what I do, and I'm good at it," I said. "It seemed the obvious choice for work, and Bliss has a population of people on fixed incomes and tight budgets."

I'd never considered becoming a private investigator. I nearly laughed. The thought had never occurred until she'd said it. Did Bliss even have a PI? Had they needed one before I arrived?

She smiled kindly. "You like to help. It's noble. I wish more people felt that way more often."

"It's the reason I get involved in the murders," I said.

"Is it?"

My phone buzzed and I started. "I'm so sorry. I must've forgotten to turn it off."

Her answering smile seemed to say, *did you?* "I can wait, if you need to take it," she said. "You can step out if you'd like some privacy."

I swiped to open the message from Louisa's number. "It's a text." I scrolled along, gasping at the photos she'd attached. "Someone smashed all her eggs. Those were for her soufflé stand."

"You need to go?" Miranda asked as I passed her on the way to the door.

"Yes." I tucked the phone into my purse and shot her an apologetic smile.

"Would you like to keep your other appointment for next week?" she asked. "I didn't cancel it when I made room for this one."

"Yes, please," I said, almost certain I was going to need it.

Her silent response as I hurried away suggested she agreed.

CHAPTER FOURTEEN

I pulled into Louisa's driveway twenty minutes later.

She was crouched beside a bucket of water near the hen house, the velvet skirt of her dress pooled around her hidden feet. "They ruined all the eggs," she said. "My hens are devastated. It was just so cruel. Who would do something like this?"

"Probably the same person who hurt Ben," I said, reaching into the bucket for a sponge. And the one who'd thrown eggs at my window. "Let me help. You should take a break."

"It's going to take all day to clean this up," Louisa said, flopping to sit on the ground, back rested against the hen house wall. The hood of her cape fell away, exposing a perfectly centered part in her pale hair and two identical French braids, complete with small bows at the ends.

She was outside cleaning smashed eggs from an adorable hen house in a velvet cape and gown. Was she even real?

"So the killer knows I'm trying to figure out what really happened, and they decide to make a big mess to annoy me?" she asked, offended and skirting disbelief.

"Pretty much. Except, I think this was meant as a threat. A message to let you know you aren't stealthy, and they see what you're doing, and you should be intimidated and stop."

"Oh," she said on a long soft breath. "I wouldn't have gotten that message."

I wrinkled my nose. "Sadly, I'm becoming accustomed to the whole routine. It's funny how often strangers in similar situations respond in identical ways." I lifted the soapy sponge to the wall and began to scrub.

"I didn't mean to drag you into this. I wasn't sure who else to call," she said. "Normally I'd reach out to Eli, but…"

"I know. Mason is supposed to try to spring him today. Don't worry about the mess. This won't take as long as you think to clean up," I promised, dunking the sponge back into the water. "Do you have a garden hose?"

Louisa handed me a towel. "Just the water pump near my garden. I brought this bucket of hot water from my kitchen."

I dragged my gaze over the land around us until I spotted a rectangle I assumed became a garden in the spring. An old-fashioned metal water pump rose from the ground nearby, a pail hanging from its handle.

"I didn't realize how much I count on Eli until he was taken away. I thought he didn't know I existed as an individual person. More like, he thought of me as one small part of a community he loves, but now that he's gone, I'm sure he knows all about me. I'm the one who always needs something. He probably thinks I'm helpless. I'm not. I just like doing things with him." Her cheeks flushed. "You know what I mean."

I smiled but didn't tell her what I thought about her and Eli, who were clearly in love already. She wouldn't believe me anyway. "Is this all that's left of the damage?" I asked, thrilled to have made an enormous difference in a matter of minutes.

"Not even close." Louisa groaned, then swept one arm out, pointer finger extended. "I started here because it seemed manageable. The soufflé stand was the real target."

I followed the direction of her finger to a building across the rolling field. What I'd assumed was an outbuilding was polka dotted with broken eggs.

"The soufflé stand?" I repeated.

I hadn't given much thought to where she planned to open her stand, but I hadn't expected it to be visible from her back door. "Can I see it?"

"Sure." She hauled herself upright while I finished removing the last of the egg mess from her hen house wall.

Then I followed her across the grass. "Did you call the police?"

"More than half an hour ago. I called them before I messaged you. You got here first and you don't even live in this town. It's easy to see how high I am on their priority list."

"Maybe they're all busy looking for Thelma or working on the murder investigation," I suggested, hoping those were truly the reasons and not that they didn't care. "Plus there are only three of them. A single car accident could cause them to be shorthanded."

She gave me a look that said she didn't think so.

The building destined to be her soufflé stand stood at the edge of her property facing a narrow dirt road. It appeared to be a small converted barn, larger than the image of a small stand I'd had in mind.

She unlatched and opened the creaky doors, then fastened them to the sides of the building, giving me a complete view of the interior. I'd had a garage this size in Atlanta. She could easily park three big trucks side by side and open their doors, though it wasn't much deeper or wider.

There was room for several tables and chairs, as well as a

small kitchen. Currently, the space was lined in stacked boxes, all of which were covered with smashed eggs.

"Someone broke the lock," she said.

"Do people know you planned to open a business here?" I asked.

"A few, plus Ben. Why?"

I pursed my lips, hating to say it but wanting to openly trade ideas. "Thelma's gone and someone's attacking with your hens' eggs. What if this isn't about Ben? What if it's about you?"

The sound of tires turned us toward the dirt road.

Mason's Jeep rocked slowly in our direction, its scowling driver visible through the windshield.

I slid a cautious look at Louisa. "He really doesn't like it when I get involved."

Louisa frowned. "Sheriff Wright doesn't want you to help me clean this mess?"

"He doesn't want me to provoke the murderer who likely made this mess."

"Oh," she said. "I don't want you to do that either."

I thought of the eggs smashed on my shop window and sighed. "Too late."

"Bonnie Balfour," Mason said, voice eerily calm as he climbed from his ride. "Why are you here?"

"I'm helping," I said.

It might've been the cool temperature, but I thought I saw a puff of steam rise from his head.

"Hi, Sheriff Wright," Louisa said. "I asked Bonnie to help me clean this up before the eggs hardened and became impossible to get off. I didn't mean to do anything wrong or get her into trouble."

"I am not in trouble," I said.

His narrowed eyes tightened slightly.

Louisa looked at him, her fair skin paling a bit further, then she flicked her gaze to me.

"He's not the boss of me," I said.

"He's the sheriff," she whispered, as if he wasn't standing three feet away.

"And not," I said gently, "my boss."

Louisa gave Mason another look, then backed up a step.

His face contorted slightly as he pushed a set of emotions I wasn't used to seeing behind the cool cop veil he liked to wear.

And I realized he'd been afraid for me.

I wondered again if his past had something to do with his distraction lately. Or if he was simply haunted by things I would never understand.

Mason turned to Louisa for her statement, then he worked the crime scene inside the building. He took photos and stayed to help us clean up when he finished.

"Did you see Eli?" Louisa asked, delivering a fresh bucket of steaming soapy water.

"Not today," Mason said, wiping egg from areas above our reach. "He was being questioned again when I stopped at the station. That's how I ended up responding to this call. The only other officer on duty is involved with a program at the elementary school this morning."

Louisa's shoulders sagged with disappointment, and she was quieter than usual until we'd finished.

I followed Mason to his Jeep an hour later. "Hey."

He turned to me, fresh intensity in his eyes. "I can't get this thought out of my head," he whispered. "You're going to be out here, asking questions, or visiting a new friend, and I'm going to get a call there's been another murder. Maybe an abduction. A drive-by shooting. A hit and run. Something. And when I get to the scene, it's going to be you."

My heart ached, and I took both his hands in mine. I

wanted to insist he was wrong, but I couldn't see the future, and no one was promised another day.

Mason had already lost one woman he'd cared about to violence, and nothing I said would ease that pain.

So, I hugged him.

He stiffened a moment before relaxing into the embrace. "Thank you," he whispered. "I'm not sleeping, and it's been a trying day. I saw your car before I saw you, and I thought this was that moment I fear most."

"I'm okay," I said. "I'd be even better if you told me why you aren't sleeping."

He rested his chin on my head but didn't answer.

"This is the second egg attack in two days," I said. "Two towns. Two women. Only one connection."

"I know," he said, holding me a little tighter. "Louisa."

CHAPTER FIFTEEN

*L*ouisa invited me in for tea when Mason left in an unexpected rush. He'd promised to reach out if he heard anything about Eli, Thelma or the case, and said he'd check in on me again as soon as he could.

I stepped into the cozy kitchen with relief, glad to be inside and finally finished scraping hardened egg yolks off the barn floor. My knees ached, and my gray dress pants were ruined.

Louisa's pretty velvet dress, on the other hand, was in perfect condition, if a little wet from the soapy water. I imagined her legs, however, were probably frozen.

She unfastened the cape from around her neck and hung it on a peg near the door, then added wood to the already burning fire and went to work on the tea. She'd been exceptionally quiet since Mason's arrival, and I wondered, belatedly, if it had anything to do with the comments she'd made about his attractiveness at my shop. I'd previously assumed she was just overwhelmed by the mess and feelings about the personal attack, but embarrassment would explain her silence as well.

Still, a tickling in my gut said there was something more.

"Bonnie?" she asked softly, interrupting my thoughts.

"Hmm?"

She set a kettle on her stovetop and adjusted the blue gas flame. Her cheeks were red when she turned to me, and a measure of guilt flashed in her eyes. "I need to tell you something, but you can't tell anyone else. You have to promise."

I felt my brows rise "You can tell me anything," I said.

"You can't tell Sheriff Wright."

I tensed, suddenly wondering if my intuition was farther off base than I'd suspected. "Why?" I asked carefully. Because if she was about to confess to Ben's murder, it wasn't something I could keep quiet.

Louisa nibbled her bottom lip, deliberating.

When she didn't continue right away, I nudged. "Is this secret the reason you were so quiet while we cleaned the soufflé stand?"

She nodded.

I gave myself another mental pat on the back for instinct, then gauged my distance to the back door in case things went south. "Did you kill Ben?"

Louisa's worried expression morphed briefly into confusion before sliding onto something caught between hurt and anger. "Of course not," she gasped. "Why would you think such a thing?"

"Just putting the possibility out there," I said, lifting my palms. "You're being unusually cagey, and I'm a little nervous."

She offered an apologetic smile. "Sorry."

"It's okay," I said, regrouping and sending up silent prayers of thanks I wasn't in a kitchen full of knives with a killer. "I can't imagine anything you want to say is worse than a murder confession, so just say it, and we'll go from there."

Her gaze flicked to the floor, then back to me. "You said Sheriff Wright didn't like it when you got involved in his murder investigations."

"That's right. Does it make you uncomfortable too? Because I'm really not trying to make things worse."

"Oh, no. It's not that at all!" She hurried across the small space to me, eyes wide and cheeks pink. She climbed onto the wooden stool at my side, a conspiratorial look in her eyes. "It's just that I am," she whispered.

"You are what?"

"Investigating," she said. "When I couldn't sleep last night, I remembered I still had a key to Ben's place from when we dated, so I went over and let myself inside."

I barked a laugh that made her jump and the donkeys bray in her yard. I opened my mouth to ask for more information, but another burst of laughter popped out.

She smiled. "You're not mad?"

"Uh, no. I'm impressed." Though I had a sneaking suspicion my therapist would be disappointed in the reaction. I should probably be concerned by Louisa's actions, or even afraid for her, given the things I'd been through. But all I felt was happiness. I'd found someone who understood me, and I liked it. "Tell me everything."

Her smile widened, and I could feel the sparks of excitement zig zag around the room.

The sparks were addictive.

"I thought there might be something at his place that could point to the killer, or at least to someone he'd recently argued with besides me. I'm guessing the police were already there, because I made a ring around the apartment without seeing anything useful. His laptop was gone, and his phone is probably at the bottom of the lake, but I found his e-reader on the nightstand." She beamed.

That wasn't where I thought her story was going, but I decided to roll with it. "What was he reading?"

She closed her eyes and made a small disappointed sound. *"How to Win Friends and Influence People*, but that's not the good part." Her blue eyes flicked open once more. "The e-reader was connected to his Wi-Fi."

I puzzled. "Okay. So—" I prompted.

"So I checked his email."

I wrinkled my nose, confused. "You knew his password?"

"No. That's the best part," she said, smile brightening. "The e-reader didn't need a password, and he was already logged into his email."

"You're kidding." I marveled and made a mental note.

E-readers can be gateways for easy digital snooping.

"There were a ton of open emails in his inbox. Most were related to the farmcation and its planning. From what I saw, the project involved a lot more than one lodge, spa and restaurant. They'd planned a mini farm, cabins, a stable with horseback riding, a lake with paddle boats, a garden, yoga, meditation and hiking on trails yet to be made. They were going to need a lot of land for all that. I took some pictures of the screens in case I needed to refer to them."

"Smart," I said, my thoughts quickly traveling to the donkeys outside. "A few families moved away from Meadowbrook, but the homes are still empty. Has anyone new shown interest, or come to walk through them?"

Louisa shook her head, then stood and moved to the refrigerator. "Do you mind if I make a soufflé while we talk? Cooking helps untangle my thoughts."

"Go for it. I do the same thing, baking cakes and cookies late at night when I should be sleeping but can't."

She gathered her ingredients and supplies with precision, then got right to work. "To answer your earlier question," she said, cracking eggs into a mixing bowl. "No one has come to see the empty homes, but that's not unusual. It takes a certain kind of person to want to live where the internet is unreliable and the cell signal is weak. We don't have satellites for television, and we rely on one another as much as ourselves for almost everything. No one expected we'd get new neighbors anytime soon."

I considered her words, which made perfect sense. But the timing of the recent moves struck me as important. "How often do families typically leave Meadowbrook?"

"Most stay," she said brightly. "By the time folks decide to trade their lives in for something simpler and more holistic, they've thought it over long and hard. Very few go back."

Yet several families had moved away at once, only shortly before a property developer was murdered. And one family had even abandoned their miniature donkeys in the process. It couldn't be a coincidence.

"Also," she added, "there was one email from an attorney in Alabama claiming his client lost his life savings after a poor investment made by Ben and Gus's company. The attorney was seeking a settlement to avoid a lawsuit. Ben hadn't responded, but I looked the guy up online, and according to public records in his county, the loss in question was followed by a divorce and a bankruptcy."

I cringed. "Sounds like cause for a grudge. People have killed for less."

She sighed. "It's too bad so many people think they can't be happy with less. Everyone just needs to find the right support system and community."

I watched as Louisa slid her soufflé pan into the oven and shut the door gently. "I need to tell Mason what you told me," I said. "But I don't have to tell him how you found out. I can say the details came up over tea and soufflé, which is absolutely true. Having all the relevant information will help him get to the bottom of this faster."

She pressed her lips together and nodded. "Okay."

"Okay," I agreed.

And thirty-five minutes later, I had the best soufflé of my life.

The next morning, I woke early, plagued by thoughts of Ben Reid's murder, poor, missing Thelma and the way Louisa had surprised me by letting herself into her dead ex-boyfriend's home looking for clues about his murder. I was especially interested in the fact Ben hadn't been straight with her, or the people of Meadowbrook, about the breadth and scope of the farmcation plans.

Why lie?

Was the answer to that question the thing that got him killed?

I stroked Clyde's fur as he wound around my ankles. We'd decided to enjoy our morning quiet time indoors again after a look at the temperature outside. There was a nice view of the lake from my bedroom, so I'd curled on the overstuffed chair with my coffee. "Lexi has the morning shift today," I told Clyde. "Which means we can take our time getting there."

He purred and rolled onto his back, stretching his kitty paws into the air and revealing his fluffy belly, which I was never ever permitted to touch.

I rose and headed for the bedroom door with my empty mug.

A six-foot mirror with elaborate gilded frame reflected my progress as I moved down the hall toward the kitchen. I'd leaned the mirror against the wall for dramatic effect, and that's exactly what I'd achieved.

I gave myself a once over, approving of what I saw. Black leggings, a red sweater dress and black flats. After ruining my favorite gray dress pants yesterday, I'd decided to stick with casual ensembles until the Cromwell investigation was over. Finding pants that fit the way I liked wasn't easy, especially when most were made for people with much longer legs and hips half as wide. I couldn't afford to lose another pair.

I left my mug in the sink and grabbed my purse and keys.

The row of fancy dresses hung in bags from a hook near my front door gave me pause. Instead of baking when I couldn't sleep, I'd tackled a set of gowns I'd volunteered to make over. They were destined for a set of high school teachers chaperoning the Valentine's Day dance. I was making strong connections at the school and had invited the ladies to Bless Her Heart for a special after-hours event. They'd selected their gowns. I'd taken their measurements and assessed their personalities, then promised to have the dresses ready by next week.

As it turned out, insomnia was great for getting ahead of schedule.

I pivoted on my toes at the thought of my other projects, one of those being Liz's grandmama's table, and headed to my garage. I made a pass through the space where most people put their cars, but I'd set up a workshop for refinishing larger pieces, like furniture, and things that needed to be sanded or painted.

The table was nearest the rollup door, ready for its trip back to What the Dickens. I'd sent Dad a text to confirm his ability to deliver the piece before book club, and he'd responded in a heartbeat, eager to help his little girl as always. I smiled at the memory. It never mattered how old I got, he was ready to assist, rescue or battle wild animals for me at the drop of a hat. Or in most cases, a text.

I was glad for the excuse to take him away from his work. I'd barely seen him or Mama in a week, thanks to the rush for flowers so close to Valentine's Day. Bud's and Blossom's Flower Farm had officially become a big deal in the floral community, and my folks were shipping fresh buds and blossoms all over the South this week and next to shops and individual consumers. I was so proud of them both, I couldn't wait to hug their necks.

The handful of other freshly sanded, painted and stenciled items in my garage had been refinished for an online boutique I'd opened at Christmastime. The companion shop to Bless Her Heart seemed like a fun way to get word out on a larger scale. I tried to keep six to ten items available at all times and concentrate on things I didn't have room for in the store.

Satisfied things were in order, I headed back toward my front door.

Before I'd opened the online shop, which had been a larger undertaking than I'd expected, my biggest project had been turning my current home into my dream space. Making that happen had taken months of blood, sweat and tears. Literally. Plus a lot of money and help from community work crews. The home had never been lived in, unless I counted the wildlife who'd nearly ruined it, despite the fact it was more than eighty years old. The place was built as a vacation destination for a wealthy man who loved his job too much to actually leave it and go fishing. But I knew a gem in the rough when I saw it.

Before I'd purchased the home, most of my time was spent opening my store, preparing the space, stocking the racks and finding customers.

Maybe Miranda was right about me chasing something.

Or maybe I just liked to stay busy. I certainly enjoyed a challenge and the internal reward of a job completed. Better yet if the job was also well done.

I learned a lot from all my projects. Big and small. Perseverance. Tenacity. Resilience. Attention to detail. Listening to my instincts. And plenty more. Sometimes I learned about my crafts. Most times, I learned more about myself.

At the moment, all I could think about were the unanswered questions taunting me from Cromwell. I didn't have the first clue about where to find a missing chicken, so I focused on something I'd learned from a recent project. Property deeds, lines and surveys were part of a public record. And Louisa said the plans she'd seen in Ben's email, for a lodge, stables, lake and cabins, would take up a lot more acreage than he'd led her and her neighbors to believe.

Did the property-investments company own that much land? Or had they planned to slowly buy out the Meadowbrook community one family at a time?

I knew exactly how to find out.

CHAPTER SIXTEEN

I dropped Clyde off at Bless Her Heart, then pointed my car in the direction of Cromwell. I crossed the city limits line a short time later, marveling at the strange mix of log trucks and SUVs hauling canoes and towing campers. It was strange how driving a few miles could feel like traveling to another planet.

I scanned the row of shops as I passed, seeking the property-investments shop where Ben had worked. The place had been closed yesterday, but a light was on today, and I made a mental note to stop by on my way back. With a little luck, Ben's partner would tell me about the farmcation plans, his relationship with Ben and the man who'd lost his life savings to a bad investment and was now suing. But first, I had some questions for the Cromwell records department.

Traffic crept along in a slow processional toward the highway, presumably for work. If the downtown area was anything to go by, there weren't enough businesses in Cromwell to employ even a tiny portion of the population unless they were all wilderness tour guides or white-water rafting trainers. In those cases, perhaps their "offices" were near but out of sight.

A flash of light drew my attention back to the property-investments office door as it opened and closed, catching and reflecting the morning sun. Mary Acres smiled as she hurried away, and I felt my jaw swing open.

What had she been doing there? Something neighborly and normal, like checking in on Ben's grieving partner? Or something nefarious like finding ways to cover her crime?

And since when did she smile?

Honk!

I started, then gaped at the rude man behind me in a giant truck with extra wheels.

"Sorry," I muttered, rolling forward when the man jerked a hand up, telling me to go.

The marshmallow easily caught up with traffic at the next streetlight, and I stifled a smirk. Being rude hadn't gotten Mr. Big Truck anywhere any faster. But it had made me want to toss a banana peel at his window.

I made a left at the next intersection and followed my GPS to the Cromwell courthouse. Like in Bliss, the sizable stone structure housed all the town's government-run offices and their courts.

I parked in a nearly full lot and hurried past a bicycle with a shiver. The outdoor enthusiasm in this town was too much for me to fathom. Forty-something degrees was far too cold for me to willingly travel on anything without a heater.

The jog up wide front steps helped warm me a bit before I pushed into the building's grand foyer.

A stooped man wearing a security guard uniform met me inside the door. He peered into my handbag, presumably in search of contraband or weaponry, before motioning me past.

I crossed the expansive marble floor to a letter board with

room numbers and searched for the records department, then I rode the elevator to the third floor.

I paused, stupefied, upon arrival.

Inside the glass office door, a female figure chatted amiably with a woman at a large cherry desk. The first woman resembled Louisa, while also looking nothing like her. A full face of makeup made the already pretty lady breathtaking, and her ensemble was professional perfection. Her golden hair was twisted into a tight bun at the nape of her neck, and fashionable dark framed glasses covered familiar blue eyes.

I peered carefully around a wall, admiring the new look while staying firmly out of sight.

Louisa's white silk blouse, black pencil skirt and cardigan were a perfect tailored fit. And she looked completely at ease in designer leather heels I'd likely break an ankle wearing.

A familiar basket with blue-and-white checkered cloth sat on the desk between her and the other woman, a gift of bribery, I suspected.

"Well," I heard Louisa say, "if you hear anything at all, I'd appreciate a call. It's of special interest to me, as you can imagine, and please let your mama know I asked about her. I'll be sure to stop by again soon to see how you liked that soufflé."

The other woman beamed after her. "Happy to help. Thank you again!"

Louisa turned to the door, giant smile morphing into something more calculated and victorious as she pushed into the hall.

I began a slow clap, and she screeched.

"What on earth!" She pressed one hand to her collarbone in shock. "Bonnie!" she stage whispered. "What are you doing here?"

"Same thing as you, I think," I said. "Except I forgot to bring something to sweeten the encounter."

She blinked, still gathering her wits, then peeked over her shoulder as her breaths slowed. "We should talk in there," she said, tipping her head toward the elevator.

I followed her inside and waited for the doors to close.

"Okay," Louisa said, turning to me with a smile. "I've been to the Chamber of Commerce, the records department and the department of parks and recreation, gathering information on the farmcation. Parks and Rec was a bust. They'd only heard rumors, nothing official or documented with them yet. The records department wasn't much more useful."

I wanted to hug her. "Keep going."

Her smile widened. "It was so much fun! Dressing up, talking to folks, asking questions and trying to read between the lines of their answers. Hoping to see some small clue that would open another door for me to enter."

I let my mouth fall open a moment, impressed by her words. "Right?"

Finally, someone got it.

Investigating was exciting. Dangerous, on occasion, but also a thrill and sometimes quite rewarding.

She nodded. "It's a rush. I felt empowered and in control."

I nodded. "Yes!"

"You want to grab brunch and talk?" she asked, still buzzing with energy.

"Absolutely."

I squinted into the sunlight as we moved onto the sidewalk a few moments later.

"We should eat at The Weathervane," she said. "They have amazing coffee and pastries, plus a few soups and sandwiches."

"Sold," I said. "Do you want to ride together?"

Louisa grinned. "It's only a couple blocks away." She

pointed in the opposite direction of my car.

I burrowed more deeply into my wool swing coat, determined to be tougher. Then I stuffed my hands into my pockets for good measure. "Lead the way."

We passed a number of small shops on the next block. Outdoor apparel stores. A military recruitment center. And a shop called The Pretty Pantry, which looked like a container store, except everything was filled with food.

The Weathervane appeared just beyond the congestion of vehicles and shoppers. Tucked away from the road, on a rolling landscape of fields and livestock. An actual weathervane creaked and spun on top of the big red barn.

A white picket fence surrounded the structure, and an old-fashioned tractor with a happy scarecrow driver greeted guests at the open gate.

"Isn't it cute?" Louisa asked, bouncing a little as she picked up speed in the café's direction. "This is where I got the idea to skip renting a space for my soufflé stand and just clean out the little building on my property instead."

I smiled as I followed her into the café, which really was amazing. And, as promised, the food didn't disappoint.

Neither did the conversation.

"So, you pretended to be with Ben's investment group?" I asked, sipping my second mug of excellent coffee, astonished at her boldness and thoroughly entertained by that surprise.

"Yup," she said. "No one suspected a thing. I looked the part and played a little dumb, so they just told me whatever I wanted to know. Everyone's always trying to be helpful. You know how that is."

I laughed. "God bless the South." Another less-pressing thing rolled through my mind, and I had to ask. "Where did you get the outfit?"

She took a long sip of her tea, gaze darting around the room before she answered. "It's mine," she said. "From before

I moved to Meadowbrook. I kept some of my old things. I couldn't help myself."

I sat back, examining the woman before me. "It's a great outfit."

She smiled. "I've always been into fashion. You wouldn't know it, living in Bliss, but around here, Eggers are an important part of the community."

"Important how?"

"We're a founding family." She traced the rim of her cup with one fingertip. "Old money. Lots of rules and ideas about what a young woman should be and do. It was a lot to manage, and I hated it. Mama says diamonds are born of coal under pressure, but I was a child, not a lump of coal. And I never wanted to be a diamond."

It didn't take long to see the former debutante before me. In hindsight, she was evident in each perfect barrel curl, her elegant strides and posture. In some ways, now that I knew her origin story, it was easier to imagine her in that life than the one I'd actually known her in. But I also understood the pressures that came with wealth and expectation.

"My family isn't wealthy," I said, "but my ex-husband's is, and while I was married, I had a good long look at their world. Many of my neighbors and friends were elitist. Hard to please. Quick to judge but slow to forgive. My time in that world was…difficult. I failed every day for nineteen years. It was kind of miserable."

She relaxed her shoulders. "It's exhausting."

"Yeah. But I left all that behind. No strings," I said, my heart breaking a little for her. "Those people weren't my family."

"Family complicates things. Which is why I traded up, for Thelma, who never judges or complains."

I wanted to comfort her but didn't have the words.

Her expression crumbled before I could change the

subject, and she dabbed her wide doe eyes with a napkin. "Sorry," she whispered. "I'm just so worried about Thelma. I keep bursting into tears at the worst times."

I reached across the table to rub my palm over her arm. "We're going to figure this out," I promised.

She sniffled and nodded. "Thelma's smart, for a chicken, but she's defenseless, and it's cold. At first, I didn't want her to have been stolen, because I thought it would be easier to find her if she was just lost. Now, I hope she was stolen, because at least she might be fed and warm."

"Something will come up that helps everything click into place," I promised, needing it to be true like I needed air.

Louisa blew out a labored breath and nodded.

I paid our bill.

We left The Weathervane in a somber companionable silence, and I struggled to think of a way to cheer up my new friend.

"Tell me more about your day of espionage," I said, circling back to something that had made her smile. "Did you say the Chamber of Commerce knew about the full scope of the planned project?"

She wet her lips, apparently willing to let me redirect her thoughts. "Yes, but according to the records department, the investment company doesn't own any large sections of land. I pulled up a listing of all properties in the company's name and sorted them by size. None were large enough for the farmcation as planned."

I burrowed more deeply into my coat as we made our ways back toward the courthouse. "I wish I'd have been with you at the Chamber of Commerce."

"Me too. Someone definitely presented the Chamber with a plan like the one I found in Ben's email. I have photos." She perked slightly. "There were professionally drawn plans on file for a massive initiative, and I got a few quick pics."

We stopped at the next corner so she could find the images on her phone.

"Here."

I accepted the device and scrolled around the complex image on screen. "This is huge. It must span one hundred acres." I checked the far sides and corners for perspective. Where did the plans begin and end? I paused on a thin blue line along the boundary edge. "What's this?"

Louisa leaned in close, turning her back to the biting wind. "I think that's the brook. Meadowbrook was named for it. It's beautiful in the spring when the rains are plentiful and the water's—" She blinked. "Wait." She took the phone back and manipulated the photo, zooming in to inspect it from corner to corner. "I can't believe it," she said, brows pinching. "This covers the entirety of Meadowbrook!"

My brows raised as I let that sink in.

"Come on." Louisa speed walked back to the lot where I'd parked and stopped at the bicycle I'd noticed on my way inside. "He lied to me," she said. "To my friends and neighbors. To all of us."

I grimaced at the bike in her hands. "This is yours?" I asked. "Do you know how cold it is today? Or that you're wearing a pencil skirt?"

"I have leggings in my purse," she said. "I have to go into the courthouse and put them on in a bathroom."

"No, you don't. I'll give you a ride home. Maybe we can find a way to get the bike into the Volkswagen."

She scanned the lot with a sigh. "Oh, my. Is that your car?"

I followed her gaze to the marshmallow a moment before she began to run in my car's direction.

Dozens of flyers covered my windshield.

Each with Thelma's name and image, bright red Xs drawn over her feathered face.

CHAPTER SEVENTEEN

I shared my next meal with Lexi. We hovered over soups and salads on the counter at Bless Her Heart, rehashing the available details on Ben Reid's murder.

Then I moved on to a retelling of the morning's flyer incident.

Lexi speared a hunk of lettuce with her plastic fork and puckered her brow. "What did Sheriff Wright say?"

I paddled hunks of broccoli around my soup, hoping not to seem concerned. "I haven't talked to him."

"What?" She tucked the bite into her mouth, eyes wide as she chewed. "You didn't call him about this?"

"I texted. He asked if I was okay. I said yes, everything else was fine and I was driving Louisa home. That was that. He responded to tell me to be careful."

I shrugged.

Lexi straightened, her expression dumbfounded. "Those flyers were definitely a threat. Or a warning, at the least."

I didn't disagree, and it wasn't like Mason not to drop whatever he was doing and come running. So, I worried again about the possibility a criminal from his past was after him.

"Nothing was damaged," I said, still going for nonchalance with Lexi. "No one was hurt. And I have no idea who was behind the whole thing, so, I sent Mason some pictures, then stuffed all the flyers into a gallon freezer bag for later. In case he wants them."

I'd had the bags and food-service gloves in my car. I kept a box of each on standby in case Gigi needed help delivering her goodies. She owned a Ford Pinto that was older than me, but her driver's license had expired when I was in middle school, and despite several recent attempts to have it reinstated, she still needed to bum rides. Gigi thought the problem was ageism on the DMV's part. I suspected it was her horrible driving.

Lexi grinned. "He must be really distracted. Wherever he is, he's definitely flipping out," she said. "He'll say you should've called the local police."

"Yeah, well, I texted the sheriff. He didn't pursue it."

Lexi chuckled darkly. "Oh, he's going to pursue it."

I made a sour face while she stuffed another forkful of salad into her mouth. "Any ideas where Thelma could be?" I asked, changing the subject. "Wild guesses are welcome. Louisa's really struggling without her, and I can't imagine losing Clyde."

Lexi paused to give the question some thought. "Have you tried asking the competition? You assume Ben's killer took her because she went missing the night he died, but maybe the two are unrelated. Louisa came here to get dresses for an upcoming judging, and she always wins. Maybe someone decided they were tired of losing, so they made sure Thelma wouldn't be present this time. She might even show up again as soon as the next competition is over."

"Huh," I said, loving the possibility Thelma wasn't injured

or worse. "I think I know who to ask about that. Good thinking."

She nodded. "Do you think you'll concentrate on finding Thelma and leave the murder alone now?"

I wrinkled my nose. "I should. Mason and my therapist have both told me to let it go."

"Are you going to let it go?"

I tilted my head over one shoulder and scrunched my face a little more. "Probably not."

Lexi turned back to her food. "Seems like a bad idea, but you do you, I guess."

I dunked the broccoli florets, having completely lost my appetite. "I wish I knew more about the man who lost his life savings to Ben's poor investment. I meant to ask the partner at his investment firm earlier, but the flyers threw me off." I swiped my phone's screen to life and turned it to face her. "This is Arthur Talbott. I looked him up online after Louisa told me his whole life fell apart following the bad investment."

She narrowed her eyes at the poorly neglected social media profile.

Arthur was in his late fifties or early sixties with a shaved head and a lot of pictures wearing a black karate gi and belt. He'd owned a dojo, which he'd been forced to close.

Lexi whistled the sound of a falling missile. "I wouldn't want to be on that guy's bad side."

I'd thought the same thing.

The temperature seemed to drop as I raised my eyes to the shop door. A familiar figure sat on a bench near the gazebo looking back.

Grant.

Beyond him, across the massive grassy oval, outside the empty storefront, the white pickup had returned. The sight was a double-decker of frustration on an already bad day.

"Can you put this in the fridge for me?" I asked Lexi, snapping the lids closed on my meal.

"Sure."

"I'll be right back." I threaded my arms into my coat and tied the belt, then marched into the day, determined to put as many troublesome things behind me as possible, starting with my ex and hopefully ending with a personal introduction to the pickup's driver. With a little luck, the driver was just someone scoping out the area and considering the purchase of shop space.

Grant looked up when I reached his side of the street, and his lips quirked on one side. He tried to squash the self-satisfied expression before I reached him, but it was too late. I already knew what he was. He made no move to stand or meet me halfway, just waited for me to come to him, like he probably knew I would if he sat here long enough. But this was better than having him inside my shop again, where the walls felt unbearably close, and we had a beef to settle.

"Bonnie," he said, feigning surprise as I took the final few steps to his side. "Change your mind about that chat?"

"No."

I fought the urge to cross my arms or take a defensive stance. Instead, I inhaled the brisk morning air, tinged with the scents of cafés I frequented and accompanied by the soundtrack of laughter I loved. A genuine smile rose on my lips when someone called to me and waved. I recognized her face, knew her name, and sincerely appreciated the timely reminder I was truly home.

"It's time for you to go back to Atlanta," I told Grant. "I'll provide the statement you want, but first you have to leave." I planned to add this conversation to whatever letter I sent. I wanted whoever received it to know I was bullied into action. "And you can't contact me again through any means."

I didn't want him in my town or in my life. He'd contaminated my space and my peace long enough. And if I could erase him from my present and future with a single note, I would cheerfully write it. Because this time I wasn't giving in to his demands; I was choosing to finish things on my terms.

Grant crossed his legs and angled slightly on his seat, hooking one elbow over the back of the slatted bench and lancing me with his cold gaze. "You're loving this," he said. "Aren't you? Lording your little sliver of power over me."

I sighed. "Just tell whoever needs the letter to reach out to me, and I'll get them what they want, after you leave," I repeated, giving emphasis to the last three words.

He performed a soft, humorless laugh, shaking his head to shame me. "You're always lecturing about kindness and compassion, but when you're asked for the simplest thing, you attach strings. Kindness with strings isn't really kindness, Bon Bon."

You would know, I thought, willfully ignoring the stupid nickname I hated.

He stood and opened his arms, as if waiting for my embrace.

I stepped back, and his brows furrowed.

"You really do belong here," he said, lowering his arms and casting his gaze around my beloved square. "I couldn't make sense of why you'd leave the life we had for this. But I suppose running a junk store in no man's land suits you."

"Bonnie!" Mason's voice rang through the air, and I spun toward it.

He headed my way with a takeout tray and two coffees, and I smiled.

Relief and joy washed through me at the sight of him. My protector and my best friend.

Who I was falling irrevocably in love with.

The truth hit like a freight train to my tender heart. The growing comfort and confidence I found in him, the strange tug of protectiveness when I sensed he was hurt or hurting. The knowledge he would never allow me so much as a papercut on his watch.

I loved Mason Wright. *Holy peach pie.*

And it felt nothing like anything I'd experienced before.

I was moving in his direction before I'd made the conscious choice. "The fastest way out of town is Highway Two," I called over my shoulder. "If you leave now, you can be home in time for dinner."

Then I released my past with both hands and any lingering fibers of myself, and I ran to my future.

Mason caught me in his free arm and kissed the top of my head. "Grant?"

"Yep."

"Did you just run him out of town?" he asked, grinning as he turned us away once more.

"Yep."

"Atta girl," he whispered, passing me the coffees and raising his free hand overhead in a final goodbye to the man he'd likely never wanted to meet.

I leaned into the strength of his side, savoring the perfect moment. Until a white pickup rolled by.

With Mary Acres behind the wheel.

CHAPTER EIGHTEEN

Gigi and Sutton held the double glass doors open at What the Dickens, while I helped Dad carry Liz's refinished table inside. Book club started soon, and three of us hadn't read a single page, but we came bearing a beautiful table, so there was that.

The gorgeous royal blue paint and gold stencil seemed to glow under the unusual bookstore lighting. I couldn't clearly see the bulbs in the bevy of old-fashioned chandeliers hung overhead, but they were all elaborate and gorgeous, throwing a golden aura over the space and flickering gently like candles.

Energy crackled in the air as we placed the revamped piece on a round handwoven rug at the center of the main sales floor. A round of oohs and aahs went up from a group of nearby shoppers.

I smiled proudly as tears welled in Liz's eyes. She slipped a finger under her retro-style glasses to capture a renegade drop.

"It's beautiful," she said. "Grandma would love this."

A few of the shoppers moved forward, running fingers

over the paint and complimenting both Liz and me on the work. Others went to the counter to check out. It was closing time, after all.

Dad kissed my cheek and said his goodbyes. He had a hot dinner waiting at home with my mom.

I promised to stop by soon and to stay safe until then.

When the door closed behind him, Sutton marched to my side and shook her head at me. "You are a mess," she said, a bevy of bangles jingling on her pale, wrinkled arms. "Gigi told me as much, but I had to see it to believe it."

I shot Gigi a look for telling folks I was a mess, then pulled Sutton into an embrace. "I am so excited to see you," I said, squeezing tight before letting go. "When are you going to give up all these little visits, move here permanently and be done with it?" I asked. "You know there's an open store-front on the square, right? Your plants would love it here."

She tipped her head over one shoulder, then the other. "I don't know. The old owner died. Seems like bad juju. The plants might be uncomfortable. You'd be surprised how persnickety some can be. Rubber trees aren't bad, but succulents are fickle. I'd almost hate to ask them. The cacti are prickly all the time, so I suppose it wouldn't matter where we lived."

I grinned. "Sounds like a yes to me."

She blew a long breath through her nose, assessing me. "I can't believe Judy let things get like this again. How is she? Are you keeping her close?"

I thought of the tiny succulent Sutton gave me last year. Sutton had promised Judy would keep me safe. "She's good," I said. "I keep her at the shop. You should stop by and visit her."

The door opened and a pair of shoppers slipped out, while Gretchen, Sutton's great-niece, stepped inside.

"Hey," she said brightly. "Sorry I'm late. I had a last-minute reading that went long, but I think love is on the way for him, so that's all good." Her smile widened as she unfastened her coat and looked at me. "I hear you're keeping life interesting."

"I try," I said. "What have you heard?"

She motioned to the trio of women wrapping up their purchases at the counter.

The ladies turned to wave, and I immediately recognized them from Grant's ambush at my shop. "My heroes," I said, nearly tackle-hugging them. "Thank you."

"Don't mention it," the shortest of the three ladies said. "It's what we do here."

The lady beside her beamed. "We stick up for each other. You do it too."

I felt the tug of belonging in my core and nodded my thanks, temporarily unable to say anything more.

Gigi joined the ladies as they collected their new books and made their way to the door. The foursome chatted warmly, as if they were old friends. Maybe they were.

They were my new friends for life.

Sutton pushed back to my side, still eyeballing the space around me. "I'm not sure what to do about you, but I've got a plant for your new friend, Louisa," she said. "I'll drop if off soon, so you can give it to her. Be sure to tell her Judy saved your life."

"Will do," I said, a fresh smile tugging my lips.

Gigi returned with a shiver, rubbing the chill of outdoors from her arms. "I've been meaning to talk to you about that. Gretchen and Sutton came over for dinner last night, and we think you should redirect the energy you're using on this murder investigation and concentrate on the HANS instead. You don't want to mess around and bumble that up."

I dragged my gaze pointedly from Gigi to Sutton, then

Gretchen, our local love guru. "I'm not bumbling anything. Things are good with Mason and me."

Good-ish, I thought, recalling the obvious secret he'd been keeping.

Things were good-adjacent.

Gretchen clucked her tongue. "You need my soul mate reading, then you'll be more careful about things."

I looked to Liz for help, but she was smiling at the restored table, as if it'd said or done something funny.

The other women all looked pointedly at me.

"Maybe we should start talking about this month's book," I suggested.

Mirabelle moved forward from the refreshment table, where she'd been noshing and listening. A light dusting of crumbs clung to her royal-blue velour track suit. "We'll get to that. First I want to know how the investigation is going."

"But—" I started.

"Nope," Mirabelle said. "Give us a rundown on the situation with Louisa Eggers. We've all gotten attached to her and Thelma while Louisa cared for her uncle. We're invested."

The others nodded, and I reconsidered the request. I didn't think Louisa would mind if I shared her story. In fact, I suspected she'd appreciate the new input, feedback and perspective these ladies might offer. So, I spilled what I knew.

The book club listened, hanging aghast on every awful word.

"Wow," Gretchen said. "I had no idea all of that was happening."

Liz sighed. "Poor Louisa must be lost without her hen. I don't even have a pet, but I talk to this mouse all the time, and I miss him when I go very long without seeing him."

I glanced nervously around the floor, hoping the mouse didn't live inside the bookstore and wondering if that was what I often saw her looking at when I didn't see anything at all.

Mirabelle returned to the refreshments table and collected a handful of cookies before collapsing onto a chair at the large oval table near the back of the shop. Mr. Dinky, her overweight Pekinese, looked up upon her return, and she passed him a cookie.

The rest of us followed her lead, filling every chair.

"I can't believe it," she said. "It's not right for Louisa to go through all of this. She's so kind and genuinely good to her core."

We shared a collective moan of agreement, and a weight hung over the room as we processed the unfortunate situation.

Gigi, Sutton, Gretchen, Liz, Mirabelle and I traded long looks.

Mirabelle leaned over the table on her elbows, eyes fixed to mine. "I'll deny it if any one of you repeats this, but Wilhelmina at the *Cromwell Chronicle* called the other day to say one of ours was over there meddling. I ignored her at the time, but I suspected it might've been you. Now I'm going to have to return her call and see if she has something of interest for us. I might have to tell her something in exchange. Tit for tat."

I sat taller, intrigued by this new info-swap possibility. "You would share information? Do you think she'll agree?"

She sighed and nodded. "I can't believe I'm saying this, but yes. I'll work with Wilhelmina, for Louisa's sake." Mirabelle's pained expression revealed the depth of her sacrifice.

Another small bridge was forming between our towns, and the thought made something in my chest wiggle. "Excellent."

We pushed our books aside, along with any pretense of

discussing it, and got down to business. An hour later, we'd made notes and charts, brainstormed and created theories from alien chicken abduction to a fowl fetish gone wrong.

In the end, we had no idea who'd want to kill Ben Reid, but the group's guesses were in line with mine. Mary, Ben's business partner, or Arthur Talbott.

Mentally exhausted, we bundled up for our trips home.

"Before we go," Liz said, following us to the door. "We really need to name this book club. I post the notice on my website and flyers every month, and we really need something a little catchier than Book Club."

My idea-well was dry, and I rarely made it to the meetings, so I waited for someone more invested to comment.

"How about Who Picked This Book?" Sutton asked. "That's the first thing everyone always asks when the new title goes up."

Gigi laughed.

"Well, it's true," Sutton said. "Unless you want something that rhymes or is more personal. Like Fiction Addiction or Book Babes."

The group exchanged uncertain looks.

Mirabelle waved us out of her way. "Let's think on it. Several members are missing tonight. We can revisit the topic next time. Now I have to walk Mr. Dinky so he doesn't have an accident."

Liz held the door for her to pass, then waved goodnight as Mirabelle and Mr. Dinky jaywalked to the square.

Sutton and Gretchen shouldered their purses, ready to brave the winter night. "As far as Ben Reid goes, my money's on the girlfriend," Sutton said. "It's always the significant other. Watch any true crime show. I'd talk to Mary if I was you. She probably has the chicken too."

Gretchen frowned. "It's not always the significant other.

Sometimes love is real, and the partners would rather die than see their other half in pain."

Gigi sighed. "It was like that with Oscar and me."

The tickle of intuition stirred in me, and I knew it was the same for Mason and me. He'd protect me at any cost, and while I was smaller and physically weaker than him, I would do the same for him.

I tried to stuff the idea aside, but my heart dug in its heels. Denying the truth wouldn't make it less true. And I needed to tell him how I felt. In the interest of transparency.

Sutton stared at me. "Trust me and talk to the girlfriend."

Gretchen sighed. "My money's on the business partner. I think money is the cause of most tragedies, not love. People are greedy and unkind when cash or power is on the line. And it sounds like that property-investments group had a lot of both at stake."

I thought again of the massive farmcation plans Louisa had turned up at the Cromwell Chamber of Commerce today. Done right, the completed project was sure to draw the interest of investors and vacationers across the country and their money as well.

Maybe Ben had wanted to scale back, or be forthright with the citizens of Meadowbrook and his partner had disagreed. Maybe the partners had come to an impasse on another matter completely. The possibilities, with stakes so high, were endless.

"I think," Gigi said, tapping a finger on the table. "You only have to ask yourself who had the most to lose, then go from there."

"Is that all?" I said, smiling at the simplistic, but accurate, breakdown.

Who had the most to lose with Ben alive?

It was the million-dollar question.

CHAPTER NINETEEN

I slid the marshmallow against the curb outside Baker & Reid Property Investments in Cromwell the next morning, then checked the time on my dashboard.

Nine o'clock sharp. And lucky me, the lights were already on inside.

The shiny black BMW SUV beside my Volkswagen gave me hope for an impromptu meeting with Mr. Baker. It seemed like the sort of high-end vehicle a property-investments person would own. And everyone else in the town seemed to drive vehicles covered in mud.

Except for Louisa and her bicycle.

I made a mental note to ring her again when I finished with Mr. Baker. She hadn't picked up when I tried her number before leaving home. I supposed she was already out tending to her hens and donkeys. My folks consistently started work with the sunrise, and they only had flowers to care for. No braying animals and horde of hens in need of sustenance.

While I was in Cromwell, I'd take Sutton's advice and have a chat with Mary. Assuming she'd have time to talk to me between accusing people of murder, which seemed to be her favorite pastime. *She'd have loved the Salem Witch Trials,* I thought, as a cold gust of wind propelled me toward the property-investments office.

I cheered internally when the door opened easily beneath my grip.

A svelte man, closer to my age than Louisa's and Ben's, stood near a side table and coffee maker several feet away, apparently waiting for the pot to brew. He straightened at the sight of me and greeted me with a small smile. "Morning," he said cordially, smoothing his light-brown hair where it had visibly thinned on top.

"Morning," I said, almost certain he was the man I'd hoped to see.

He wore tan pants and loafers with a blue button-up shirt and coordinating pinstriped tie. "Can I help you?" he asked, searching me with curious brown eyes when I didn't say more.

"Hi. Sorry," I said. "I'm Bonnie Balfour. I was just gathering my thoughts." I paused, unexpectedly nervous and wishing I'd given more thought to what I'd say before waltzing inside.

His smile grew. "Come on in, Bonnie. I'm Gus Baker. It's nice to meet you."

A zing of victory bounced in my chest. *It was him.*

"Hi, Gus."

He set his hands loosely on his hips, striking a casual pose. Amusement played on his thin lips. "Are you looking to purchase a local property?" he guessed. "Maybe make an investment of some kind?"

Definitely not, I thought, imagining a black cloud over the Baker & Reid office. Bad luck plagued this place. First losing Arthur Talbott's life savings, then losing a partner to murder.

I didn't want any of their bad mojo to rub off. I had enough troubles of my own.

What I needed was a plan.

"I'm a friend of Louisa Eggers," I said, deciding on the truth. "I was very sorry to hear about what happened to Ben."

Gus's smile fell, and his hands dropped against his sides. "You knew him?"

"Only through Louisa, but it was such a terrible thing. I'm sure you're devastated."

Gus heaved a sigh and tipped his head toward a small seating arrangement near one wall. An office door stood open on each side. "Can I get you anything?" he asked. "Water, coffee?"

"No, thank you."

He motioned to a love seat, then lowered onto an armchair and waited for me to sit. "Ben's loss has devastated everyone who knew him," he said. "He will truly be missed."

He sounded like a generic funeral soundbite. And didn't appear upset at all.

"I don't think the loss has fully hit me yet," he said, clearly reading my mind. "It still seems too impossible to be real."

I nodded. "Of course."

Gus rolled his shoulders back and cleared his throat. "Is there anything I can do for you since you're here?"

I set my purse on my lap and gripped the sides, determined not to fidget. "I'd love to hear about the farmcation project you had planned for Meadowbrook, if you have time," I said. "What Louisa described sounds lovely. When do you anticipate moving forward?"

Gus frowned. "I'm afraid that project is no longer viable without Ben. He was the one with connections to the surrounding community, which, as you know, is…unique. He was the one with personal access to the people, and he'd been the one laying all the groundwork. Without him, the farmcation is a non-starter." He unclasped and reclasped his hands, as if to say, oh well.

"I see," I said, not sure I saw at all. "Do you mean Ben had formed the relationships necessary to purchase all of their homes?"

Gus parted his hands again and patted them on the arms of his chair, evaluating me now. "Ben was building bridges within the community. Meadowbrook's acceptance was necessary for the farmcation to succeed. We couldn't expect guests to pay top dollar for a peaceful rural vacation, then surround them with dozens of unhappy hicks."

My brows rose, and I suppressed my urge to retort.

His eyes widened, and he dragged a hand down his face. The sudden loss of composure had surprised him too. "Look," he said, backpedaling. "I'm sure those people are fine. Kind. Nature lovers. Whatever. We didn't need all their houses. And none of it matters anymore anyway. Ben's death put a stop to the whole thing. So, the Meadowbrook folks can just go back to bathing in horse troughs and dressing like it's eighteen hundreds Oklahoma. It's irrelevant to me. And you, if you were hoping to get a piece of the project. Now, if you'll excuse me."

The front door opened, and a man in a gray suit entered, unfastening the button on his suit jacket as he headed in our direction, brow furrowed. His eyes flashed as they moved from me to Gus then back.

Gus rose with a grimace. "I've got a client of my own to mend fences with."

I froze, temporarily immobilized by the icy stare of Arthur Talbott.

Even without his karate gi, there was no mistaking him. Something in his posture and stride demanded respect and exuded control.

Gus met him outside an open office door, and I wondered

what the fit, unhappy man was capable of when he lost control.

The pair shook hands and entered the office without so much as another look in my direction. And Gus closed the door behind them.

I saw myself out.

I climbed back into my car and took a minute to roll the new information around in my mind. Was Gus Baker guilty of murder or just of being a judgmental jerk? And why was Arthur Talbott meeting with him now?

Maybe Mary could shed some light. She'd been smiling when she left his office yesterday.

And I wasn't anywhere close to smiling now.

I made the trip through town with ease, then turned onto the path into the woods with a smile. Meadowbrook was becoming one of my usual haunts, and I hoped that might remain true after Ben's murder was solved.

Community members waved as I piloted the marshmallow through the forest, pausing in their chores to welcome me.

I slowed outside the home where I'd seen Mary smirking on the day Eli was hauled away, and I pulled in a ragged breath.

The small white pickup truck I'd seen on the square and outside my storage unit sat in the driveway.

It took some serious internal convincing to haul myself out of the car, but ultimately I got the job done.

"Bonnie Balfour," someone called as my car door shut, scaring me half-witless.

"Glory," I whispered, pressing my back to the car and attempting to look less frazzled than I felt.

Mary moved along the side of her home, eyes narrowed

and lips tipped in a knowing grin. A long wool cape hung from her shoulders to mid-calf, covering her ensemble completely, save for two tall brown boots disappearing beneath the hemline. "I wondered how long it would take you to come here. The infamous amateur sleuth from across the great divide."

I stiffened slightly, not particularly thrilled with her choice of adjectives. I was hardly infamous.

The soft, repetitive clucking of chickens pulled my attention to the grass behind her. A cloud of black-and-white barred hens pecked and scratched the ground, their patterned feathers giving the impression of stripes. A dozen zebra-chickens—or hens wearing old-fashioned prisoner garb.

I watched the group as it moved, searching it for signs of Thelma, and wondering if one of these birds was the one who always came in second to Louisa's prized hen.

Mary's dark brows knitted together as she drew nearer. "Are you here to ask me about Ben's murder? Or Thelma's disappearance? And while I'm asking the questions," she said, "why do you even care? Who are you? No one around here had ever heard of you until the night Ben died."

I opened and shut my mouth before deciding to skip all the niceties and return her extreme directness. "I'm here because I'm a friend of Louisa's and her uncle's. I want to know what makes you think Louisa or Eli would hurt Ben."

Her expression darkened, and she crossed her arms.

"I might be new here," I admitted, "but I can't imagine Louisa or Eli are capable of anything as heinous as murder. So, it'd be nice if you had some information to support your accusations. You owe Eli that much. He's stuck in jail because of what you said."

Mary's lips twitched, then spread into a sly grin. As if she knew a big secret. One she'd never tell. "They aren't what they seem, you know. Louisa and Eli," she clarified. "She's not the precious, docile baby deer everyone thinks she is, and for the record, Eli isn't in jail. He's home. He's also quite capable of all kinds of things. You should ask him about his many talents sometime."

"What does that mean?" I asked, scanning the lane of adorable cottage-style homes, glad to hear Eli had been set free.

"Ask him," she said. "I don't want to be the one to burst your sweet little bubble."

I doubted that was true, but I pressed on, leaving the condition of my bubble alone for now. "How well do you know Gus Baker?" I asked, taking back control of the conversation. "You seemed pretty happy when I saw you leaving his office yesterday."

Mary stiffened, and I smiled, pleased that I'd hit a nerve.

"Is there something going on there?" I asked, formulating a number of possible scenarios in my mind. Maybe her relationship with Ben's partner was the key to this case.

Was it possible Ben Reid's murder was the result of something as cliché as competition over a woman?

"No," she scoffed. "Of course not."

I eyed her closely, looking for the lie.

What if romantic jealousy was the motive, but I was looking at the wrong love triangle for my suspect? Maybe it wasn't Mary, Ben and Gus, but Louisa, Ben and Eli.

And what had Mary meant about Eli? Louisa had described him as guarded and brooding. She assumed he was driven to Meadowbrook by a painful past. But what if the reason was something else entirely. Something sinister. What if Ben had learned Eli's secret and used it as leverage against him, over Louisa or the farmcation?

I pressed a palm to the side of my spinning head to pump the mental brakes. There were too many questions and not enough facts. Not to mention I was too far removed from the players to make any sense of the information I gathered. I'd need Louisa's help to filter and sort it all. Which brought me to another thing I wanted to ask Mary.

"What do you think happened to Thelma?" I asked. "Who would take her, and where could she be?"

Mary wrinkled her freckled face in disgust. "How would I know that?"

"You know hens," I said, waving a hand at the flock gathered at her feet. "I thought you'd have some insight. Is it true your hens come in second place to Thelma every year? That has to be frustrating."

She blinked. "It is."

"Her absence is kind of nice for you. Having your competition removed means your hens might have a chance at the blue ribbon now."

Mary's stunned expression darkened. "Those judges pick favorites. It has nothing to do with the quality of our hens, and Louisa knows it. I've told her so, and she still shows up to every event, making sure no other chicken farmer can get any notoriety. This is exactly what I was talking about. She pretends to care and says she wants what's best for our whole community, but when it comes down to it, all she cares about is herself, her hen, and those blue ribbons."

I frowned, unable to get riled up over ribbons.

"If she has such a big heart," Mary carried on, "then why is she more worried about her missing hen than her dead ex-boyfriend? Thelma's just a chicken for goodness' sake. Ben is a human, and he is dead!" Tears swam in Mary's eyes, and her hands curled into fists at her sides.

The plume of black-and-white chickens grew agitated, puffing and clucking more fervently, as if sensing their caregiver's dismay.

I took a step back.

"I mean," she croaked, tears falling and hands waving in my direction, "she hired you to cross enemy lines just to hunt for her hen."

The sudden change of mood made me squirm.

"I'm just a friend," I said. "I wasn't hired to do anything. And there's nothing anyone can do about Ben, aside from find his killer, which the police are working on. Thelma could be hurt and need help. Of course Louisa is trying to get her home safely. Wouldn't you do the same?"

Mary gasped, as if I'd slapped her. "Right," she said sharply. "The police are working on it." She made air quotes as she threw my words back at me. "You mean your boyfriend, the sheriff, is helping. Because Louisa's involved, and the whole world tilts on its axis to lean in her direction."

I rolled my eyes dramatically, barely able to keep up with her myriad complaints.

Clearly her issues were with Louisa, and whatever they were, they ran deeper than the blue ribbons. Coupled with her temper, I couldn't help wondering if she'd killed Ben in a fit of pique over him casually speaking his ex's name.

"I hear Ben was a big fan of Thelma's," I said. "He was suing for partial custody. Did you know that?"

Her expression cleared a moment before she barked an ugly laugh. "Of course I knew. I tried to talk him out of it, but Ben was an idiot! He got life insurance on her while he was dating Louisa for crying out loud! Dumb! Dumb! Dumb!"

A few neighbors lifted their gazes in our direction, pausing in their yardwork to take note of Mary's outrage.

At least there would be witnesses when she imploded.

I jerked my attention back to her, in case she lashed out while my head was turned.

And she burst into tears.

"Uhm." I glanced back to the onlookers, and they looked away.

Traitors.

"I am so sorry," she said, forming each word on a sharp inhale. "I have big feelings," she wailed. "And all of this has just been too much."

"We'll get it all figured out," I said cautiously. "Don't worry."

She nodded and turned away, heading for her home.

I waited, unwilling to go inside. Just in case the tears were a ruse.

She sat on her porch step and pulled a wad of tissues from an apron beneath her cape and tried to dry her eyes. "Louisa never cries," she said. "She's always perfectly put together. Every last hair. Even her ridiculous eyelashes."

"Louisa isn't perfect," I said. She was just very good at putting up a good strong front, probably the results of her breeding and a whole lot of debutante classes. Cami still drew on her childhood lessons when faced with a particularly awful person or event. "She's human, like the rest of us. We're all struggling more than others think."

Mary looked up at me, small and defenseless beneath her tears. "Ben and I weren't really dating. We spent a lot of time together because I was helping him with the farmcation plans. I let Louisa think we were dating because I wanted her to see I was just as fantastic as she was. I could get the same guy she did." Mary released a shuddered breath, and her eyes unfocused a little. "The farmcation was going to make things better around here."

"How?"

"Money." She gave a small humorless laugh. "The project would've brought a lot of money into Meadowbrook. I don't know how the rest of these guys survive on no income, trading favors and homegrown produce, but I've got bills that didn't go away just because I dropped off the grid. Don't get me wrong. I love the cottagecore life, but it's hard. And I need an income. Ben was going to put me in charge of events and activities planning. I would've had healthcare."

"I'm sorry," I said.

She huffed a small laugh. "Me too. I sold everything I owned when I came here. Now I have no money and couldn't go back if I wanted."

I thought again of the empty homes on Louisa's lane. Had those families felt the same way? If so, had they jumped at the chance to sell to Ben so they could start over outside Meadowbrook?

"Is that why you were at Ben's office yesterday? Hoping to get the farmcation going so you could have the job Ben promised?"

She looked away. "I tried, but he wasn't interested. He said he was glad to put the project to rest. He thinks Meadowbrook would bring in more money as a golf course. I told him I was glad to help however I could, even on a project outside Meadowbrook, but I don't think he'll call."

"A golf course?"

She nodded. "That could never happen, unless everyone here suddenly decided to leave. Fat chance of that. The people here are obsessed, especially Mrs. Pankin, and everyone follows her like she's some maternal icon."

"I met her," I said. "She helps Louisa with the donkeys."

"She helps everyone," Mary said, softening. "She's a good person. She's always telling me to spend more time in meditation, commune with nature or work physically until I sweat—all ways to manage my feelings."

"Sounds reasonable," I said, thankful my therapist hadn't prescribed any of that. Probably because she knew I'd fail miserably. Or have a stroke. "Did Ben ever mention a man named Arthur Talbott?"

Her dark brows rose. "How do you know about that guy?"

"I saw him at the office today when I went to speak with

Gus."

She considered me a moment. "He lost a lot of money on an investment with Ben, and he blamed Ben, but Ben said it was a joint decision and Arthur understood the risk. He was harassing Ben about it, even though there wasn't anything to be done on the matter now. The money was gone."

I nodded, stepping away. Her truck caught my eye as I turned. "Were you in Bliss yesterday?"

Her green eyes widened. "I went to see the lady everyone says can name a person's soul mate. I shopped a bit and ate while I was there. Was that a problem?"

I shook my head. As long as she wasn't stalking me, I didn't care how much time she spent in my town.

But why had she been in my town all those times? And at my storage unit?

"It's nicer than folks in Cromwell admit," she said. "I went there half expecting to wade through trash and pray the buildings didn't crumble around me. Instead, I spent a whole afternoon checking things out."

I frowned at her description of my town, as she'd assumed it would be. What did people in Cromwell tell each other? Where had she gotten such awful ideas?

My phone buzzed, and a text from Mama appeared. I lifted a finger to indicate I needed a second to check the message, just in case something was wrong, then smiled at the words. Mama was planning an after-party for Gigi's grand opening on Valentine's Day, and I was invited to help out.

"Here's my number in case I can help you again," Mary said, pulling my attention back to her as she retrieved a business card shaped like a hen from her apron.

I accepted the card, then returned to my car.

I'd either made a new friend or invited a killer for a visit.

The way my days were going, it was anyone's guess.

CHAPTER TWENTY

*L*ouisa was on her front porch with Mrs. Pankin when I arrived. Both ladies were bundled in adorable, but warm-looking frocks, clearly not planning any serious lawn or animal care in the near future. Louisa's blond curls bobbed against her simple black coat as she swept the porch. Mary Janes and cream tights complemented her burgundy-and-cream print dress beneath. Mrs. Pankin knocked spider webs away from the porch corners and ceiling, careful to dodge falling debris.

The women stopped to wave when I climbed out.

"Bonnie!" Louisa beamed. She set her broom aside and hurried to meet me in the driveway. "What are you doing here?"

"Just visiting," I said. "I had some time before work and a whole lot of questions."

Her smile faltered at that. "Come on in. We can talk."

"I'll put the kettle on," Mrs. Pankin said warmly before turning to head inside.

She was busy in the kitchen when we arrived a moment later. Louisa's kettle sat on the stovetop waiting to boil, and a fire roared in the fireplace. "Sit," Mrs. Pankin said. "I've got this covered."

Louisa and I stripped off our coats and hung them on knobs by Mrs. Pankin's wrap, then eagerly obliged.

"We were just talking about you," Mrs. Pankin said, setting a trio of cups and saucers on a tray. "I hope you're well."

"I am," I said, sighing softly. "I've been trying to work through the things we know about Ben's death and Thelma's absence, but every answer I get just leads to more questions. Any chance you have time to weigh in?"

Louisa's expression lit up. "Of course. Thank you for keeping this whole thing going. I tried to get to the bottom of it, but I gave up when I didn't get anywhere."

"I've never been one to let anything go," I said. "It's a curse."

"Well," Mrs. Pankin said, "let's see if we can help."

I started talking, and the words kept coming until we finished an entire pot of tea.

Mrs. Pankin put on a second.

The women nodded as I told them about my visits with Gus and Mary, cringed at my concerns about the man who'd lost everything thanks to Ben's poor investment, then gaped like fish out of water when I mentioned the possible golf course.

"A golf course!" Mrs. Pankin said, hand trembling as she set her cup on her saucer. "How awful. What about all these beautiful trees? Some are two hundred years old! They'd knock them down so a bunch of rich old men can play ball?"

"Priorities," I said, fully understanding the value of a good tee time to a businessman.

Louisa traced the rim of her cup with one finger. "Arthur Talbott met with Gus today?"

I nodded. "He lost his life savings, his wife and his business to a bad investment with Ben, had traded emails with Ben about a settlement, and now he met with Gus."

Mrs. Pankin tapped her spoon gently against her saucer. "Persistent."

"He has definite motive," I said. "And anyone who could lift a rock, or something similar, had means, judging by the wound on Ben's head."

I hadn't gotten a close look at the actual injury, but I'd seen the blood and general damage from several feet away and overheard the coroner commenting on how the weapon was probably at the bottom of the lake with a thousand stones just like it.

"Arthur's definitely a suspect," Louisa said.

"One of my top three," I said, thinking of Gus and Mary. "Which reminds me. I heard Eli's home. Have you seen him?"

Mrs. Pankin nodded. "He was released last night, and he's been hard at work on his property all day, chopping wood and making up for the days he lost. As far as I know, he hasn't spoken to anyone. Folks have stopped by to take him meals, but he just thanks them and keeps working."

Louisa looked deflated, and I wondered if she was one of the folks who'd dropped by with a meal and been ignored.

Mary's successfully planted seeds came back to mind, and I imagined him as the villain, allegedly capable of all sorts of ugly things. The manual labor reminded me of Mrs. Pankin's advice to help Mary manage her emotions. If I were Eli, I'd have plenty of rage after being held at the police station for three days.

"Any idea what Eli said to threaten Ben?" I asked, recalling the Cromwell officer's reasoning for taking him away.

Mrs. Pankin wet her lips and leaned closer to the table. She cast a quick look in Louisa's direction before locking eyes with me. "I heard Ben offered to buy Eli's property, and he said no. So, Ben tried to blackmail him, and that was when Eli raised his ax onto his shoulder, implying without words that Ben was in immediate danger if he didn't leave."

Louisa's eyelids closed briefly. "I heard something like that too. I hoped it wasn't true."

"I think it was," Mrs. Pankin said. "It sounds right. Eli wouldn't want to sell his property, and he doesn't seem the sort to negotiate or tolerate bullies."

Louisa poured another cup of tea, and I sensed the topic switch before she spoke. "Mary said Ben took out an insurance policy on Thelma?"

"Yeah," I said with a slight wince. "Sorry. That was really awful of him, but it's a thing some folks do with valuables. My ex-husband kept policies on all sorts of things."

"Why?" Louisa asked.

"I guess he wanted to be sure he was reimbursed financially if anything ever happened to any of them." I frowned, realizing how badly that made things sound for poor Thelma.

Louisa paled and raised a hand to cover her trembling lips.

"Oh, no. Louisa," I said. "I'm not suggesting—" I looked to Mrs. Pankin for help.

She gave Louisa's hand a motherly pat.

"Maybe you can figure out which insurance company he used and call them," I suggested. "Ask about the policy."

Louisa nodded, brightening slightly with new purpose. "I can do that. Gus might even know."

I smiled. "That's the spirit. Meanwhile, how's everything else going?"

"I haven't been able to concentrate on much. So, I've been working on small projects around the house and waiting for an epiphany about Thelma's location. Or maybe a visit from

Eli. I'd hoped he might come over and let me know he was okay."

Mrs. Pankin offered a sad smile, then rose and carried her cup to the sink. "I'm sure he'll be around soon. As for me, I think it's time I took Jack and Jill the apples I promised." She smiled as she wrapped her narrow body back into the wool-lined coat. "I'll see you next time, Bonnie. And I'll check on you again this evening, Louisa, when afternoon chores are done."

"Thank you," Louisa said, watching her friend disappear through the back door.

I smiled over the rim of my teacup. "Why don't you stop by Eli's place in the morning and take him a soufflé," I suggested. "Catch him before he gets started on his chores, when he's fresh from sleep."

She chewed her lip. "I wouldn't want to ambush him, or make him feel pressured if I just showed up with it hot and ready like that. He might not even eat breakfast."

"Trust me." I grinned. "Eli will be thrilled to see you, and he will gladly eat your quiche. It's hardly an imposition. Besides, friends check on one another."

"I suppose that's true." "It is," I assured.

Her gaze darted through the room, and I could practically see the mental wheels turning as she considered the possibility. "I'll bet he overheard a lot of details on Ben's murder investigation while he was stuck at the police station all that time. I could ask him about that while I'm there."

"Excellent," I said. "We can use all the information we can get."

"Agreed." Her blue eyes snapped back to mine. "I can stop by your shop tomorrow for lunch and tell you what I learn."

"That's perfect. I actually expect to have a gift for you by then. Gigi's friend Sutton is delivering a special plant for you.

Sutton talks to plants and animals, and she says this one will help protect you."

I waited for her laughter.

Louisa illuminated. "That sounds wonderful! I'll bring a thank-you note for you to pass back to her!"

"She'll love that."

"It's a date," Louisa said, and I smiled.

Because tonight I had a date with a sheriff.

I hurried home after work, making the drive through town at just above the speed limit, then moving a little faster as I got closer to the lake. I was eager to shower, change and get to Mason's in time for dinner. He'd stopped by Bless Her Heart to finalize plans earlier, and it was all I'd been able to think about since then. I only hoped I could find the right words to tell him I'd bumbled around and fallen in love with him. An admittedly silly and wistful problem better suited for people half my age, not ones pushing forty and recently divorced.

Falling in love was for youthful, carefree folks. Far too dangerous for my long-battered heart.

So why did loving him make me happy instead of terrified?

The familiar shape of his Jeep came into view as I approached my driveway, as if I'd somehow conjured him with my frantic thoughts.

I parked and took my time climbing out, gathering my wits and words. Then, I realized he might've come by to cancel our plans.

"Hey," he said, meeting me at the front of my car and pressing a kiss to my cheek. "How are you?"

"Okay," I said. "Unless you're here to cancel, then I'm a little bummed."

"Only a little?" He went to the passenger side of my car and pulled Clyde's carrier into his arms.

I watched him, attempting to read his mind and guess his motives. "Are you canceling?"

"Nope."

"Good." I smiled. "I hope you brought dinner, because I didn't plan on cooking."

He tipped his head and shot me his trademark be-serious expression. "I've got pad Thai and chicken riding shotgun."

"Bless you." I led the way onto my porch, then let us inside. Mason set Clyde free while I turned on the lights and shucked off my coat.

"Be right back," he said, heading out once more, presumably to retrieve our dinners.

A few minutes later, Clyde was fed and Mason and I were tucking into our meal, glasses of water at the ready. We liked our pad Thai spicy.

"What made you decide to eat here tonight?" I asked. "Everything okay at your place?"

He smiled. "I was in a hurry to see you. Maybe even looking for excuses to expedite the process, and I realized you come to my place more often than I come to yours these days. That didn't seem fair, and your place is nicer." His eyes sparkled. "I already had dinner with me, so I decided to come here and wait for you instead."

I smiled, enjoying the rush of warmth and butterflies through my body as he spoke.

"I'd say I don't know why we spend so much time on the boat," he continued, "but I suppose it's because you're trying to slowly redecorate for me, one new thing at a time."

A surprised laugh bubbled past my lips. "You noticed, huh?"

His get-serious expression was back in a flash. "I'm literally a detective. Like for a living. You don't think I'd notice a thick white towel set in my bathroom, where the threadbare navy one belonged? Or a bamboo charcuterie board on my countertop."

"I'm not sure what I love more," I said, intentionally breathless. "That you know what a charcuterie board is or how to properly pronounce it."

Mason's expression grew serious, and he leaned in for a gentle kiss. "I like when I find your little changes. It reminds me that you care and think of me when we aren't together, that you think I have the potential to not be such a dude, and that you're invested in that transition. The least I can do is embrace the process."

"You're not mad?"

He slid his fingers against the sensitive skin of my neck and curled them in the hair at my nape. "It's one of many things I've come to love about you," he said.

I stared back, lips parted, soaring high on that seemingly innocent statement and reading between the lines. "So you came because you couldn't wait to see me," I said.

He kissed me again before returning to his meal. "That, and I don't want you driving home alone again after dark or walking to your door alone when there's a killer on the loose. Especially not while I'm already home, safe and sound. I should be the one commuting right now, not you."

I smiled. "Very chivalrous."

"I'm a chivalrous guy."

"A definite keeper, I think."

"I should hope so," he said. "You gave me a charcuterie board."

I laughed again, feeling lighter and more like myself than I had in a while. "All right. New subject. Any luck on the Ben Reid murder case?"

"Yep," he said, smiling as he stuffed a pile of pad Thai into his mouth. "Things are moving along nicely for me on that one. How about your missing chicken?"

"She's still gone, but I had an interesting day."

Mason wiped his mouth and took a breath. "How so?"

I filled him in on my chats with Mary and Gus, seeing Arthur Talbott at the property-investments office, then tea with Louisa and Mrs. Pankin while we finished our meals.

Mason frowned. "I thought you were only after the chicken."

"Not necessarily. I want to find Thelma, but I think the two cases are connected. How do you feel about Arthur Talbott as a suspect?" I asked, recapping his reasons for being on my list.

Mason shook his head. "Talbott and his family were in Tallahassee for a wedding at the time of the murder. I've got plane tickets, photographs and two hundred witnesses to confirm it."

"Oh." I slumped a bit, torn between being thankful to narrow my suspect list and disappointed I hadn't known. Why didn't more men update their social media accounts?

"Why don't we divide and conquer on this," Mason suggested. "You look for the chicken, and I'll arrest the killer."

I wrinkled my nose. "You have to arrest the killer. I can't."

He made a comically bland expression.

"Come on," I urged. "Hasn't anything I've said helped you with your investigation at all?" I carried my empty plate to the sink.

"I wouldn't say that," he said. "Even if it was true." He delivered his plate to the sink too and grinned. "You'd use something like that against me forever."

"Would not." I laughed, enjoying his use of forever more than I should.

"Would," he said. "Anyway, I have things under control, and you can give it a rest."

"We'll see," I said, tugging the gold hoops from my ears. "I'm going to change. Meet you on the couch in five minutes?"

Mason's eyes lit with mischief. "You're going to give me a chance to change your mind?"

I laughed as I walked away. "Never."

I heard water in the kitchen sink as I headed for my bedroom and knew the space would be spotless when I returned. Because Mason was like that. And I was lucky.

He was on the couch when I returned. The kitchen clean. He patted the cushion beside him, and I slid into the spot beneath his raised arm, dragging a blanket off the back to cover us.

"Have I told you how distracted you've seemed lately?" I asked. "I think it's more than the recent murder. I noticed it months ago. Whatever it is, you can talk about it with me, you know."

Mason stiffened slightly. "I know." He glanced down at me. "I don't mean to be distracted. I'm still adjusting to my new life here. My new roles. Letting go of old ones."

"Okay," I said, getting a strange vibe from his tone and feeling myself tense in response.

"What do you think is going on?" he asked, likely sensing my tension the same way I felt his.

"I don't know. Something."

He shifted for a better look at me. "You brought it up," he said gently. "Something's obviously bothering you. Let's talk it through. What do you think is bothering me?"

"Are you involved with a secret investigation of some kind?" I asked.

His brows furrowed. "No. Like what?"

I couldn't tell if he was lying, and I felt instantly awful for pressing, but I had to know. "If you had reason to believe The Investors were coming for you, you'd tell me, right?"

Mason's expression became tender, and he pulled me onto his lap, resting my back against the arm of the couch and draping my legs over his so he could better face me. "I'm fine. I promise. No one's coming for me."

"Are you sure?"

He smiled. "As much as I can be. I love that you worry about me, but I don't have any reason to believe I'm in danger. And if I ever think something from my past is coming for me, I promise to tell you as soon as I know."

"Really?"

"Yeah," he said softly, tucking a swath of my hair behind one ear. "I'd have to, because the best way for anyone to hurt me would be to come for you. I won't allow that. I will never hurt you or knowingly put you in danger. That's a promise."

My body sagged in relief, and I leaned into his chest.

"Okay?" he asked.

"Okay," I said.

"Anything else you want to talk about?"

I smiled, sitting up again. "It's a lot harder than I expected to work on an investigation in another town," I said.

He groaned. "We're back to this again."

"Traveling is a hassle, plus I hardly know anyone in Cromwell. The whole thing is kind of a pain. I'll be glad when it's over."

"I know how you can make it stop right now."

"Solve the case?" I guessed.

"No. Stop mucking around in my work."

Clyde leapt onto the couch and curled beside us. Mason set a hand on his back, stroking Clyde's sleek black fur.

"You know what would help?" I asked, speaking the thought as it came to mind. "If Cromwell had its own amateur sleuth."

"Please don't say you want the job," Mason begged. "You'll have to close your shop if you take on two towns' worth of things that aren't any of your business."

I laughed and shoved his ridiculously toned chest. "Not me. And if there were two of us, she and I could coordinate efforts, like Mirabelle at the *Bliss Bugle* and Wilhelmina at the *Cromwell Chronicle*."

"Good grief." Mason rolled his head against the back of my couch. "The geriatric crime reporters are partnering up now? That's definitely going to lead to trouble."

"I love it. Haven't you heard? Teamwork makes the dream work."

And Louisa Eggers was shaping up to be a great teammate.

CHAPTER TWENTY-ONE

*B*usiness at Bless Her Heart was busier the next day, likely a result of the calendar's steady move toward Valentine's Day. Popular purchases flipped overnight from festive holiday-themed décor to dresses, jewelry and gifts. Those who'd planned to decorate apparently had that under control, and now the rush was on to find the perfect items for the big day itself.

Lexi hustled from dressing rooms to racks, trading sizes for customers behind the curtains.

I rang the register between bouts of restocking and tidying shelves.

Clyde prowled the store, Thelma's little feather in his mouth. His preoccupation with the feather had begun to worry me. All his other trinkets and stolen items—Clyde was a notorious acquirer of interesting objects—were hidden in corners and under rugs. The feather had become a near constant, and I got the strange idea he might be as worried about the funny little hen as I was.

The door swung open as I straightened the window display, setting the overhead bells to jingle. "Welcome to

Bless Her Heart," I called, spotting Sutton as I spoke. "Oh! Yay! I'm so glad you made it."

She stumbled inside under the weight of a wide, shallow terracotta bowl. A stout green cactus grew at its center, a single pink flower on its head. Dirt and rocks made up the rest of the seemingly too-large landscape. "Goodness," she cried, stumbling the rest of the way to my counter. "This little peanut sure is heavy." She set the pot between a fresh bouquet my parents had delivered after breakfast and Judy. "Hello, Judy," she said to the plant.

I slid around to the business side of the counter as a customer approached.

The young man gave Sutton a curious look, then handed me his credit card while she caught her breath.

I finished the transaction and assured the man his wife would adore her new antique broach and pearls, both from an estate sale in the next county. "History is so important," I assured. "And don't forget to stop at Oh My Goodies Valentine's Day morning," I told him. "You can pick up something sweet as well."

Sutton leaned in the man's direction. "Don't ever let anyone tell you flowers and chocolates are cliché. They are not. They are tradition."

He smiled, swinging his attention back to me. "History," he said.

"Exactly."

I waved goodbye, then turned to Sutton before anyone else needed to check out.

"You know," I said, circling back to her earlier complaint. "I don't think it's the cactus that's heavy. I think it's the giant pot of dirt and rocks."

She surveyed the items in question with a frown. "No. I'm sure it's Peanut."

"You named the cactus Peanut?"

Her brows puckered further with confusion. "I didn't name him."

I blinked, then rerouted my thoughts away from that particular rabbit hole. "I texted Louisa after you called this morning. I let her know you were bringing the plant, and she was delighted. She's running a few errands, then meeting me for lunch. She'll be thrilled to catch you. Can you stay a bit?"

Sutton's gaze flicked to the floor and back. "Oh, dear." She checked her watch, then the cactus. "He told me I should hurry, but I was having such a lovely time in the park."

I followed her gaze to Peanut, debating whether or not to ask for more information.

"It wasn't until the trees began to whisper that I listened," she said, concern growing with the words. "They brought the message all the way across the lake, and they don't usually work that hard for one person. She's either very special or the situation is dire. I assumed it was the latter, but I suppose it could be both."

I glanced from the cactus to the woman before me. "I'm sure everything's fine. She'll be here any minute."

Sutton shook her head as another customer approached the counter.

I rang her up and sent her off with instructions to visit Oh My Goodies, then smiled at Sutton, still visibly fretting and making odd faces at the cactus. "Do you want to grab lunch with us? I'm sure Louisa won't mind, and we can see if Gigi's free."

"It's nearly four," Sutton said. "I've already had lunch with Gigi. Hours ago."

"What?" I gasped, grabbing my phone from beneath the counter to check the time.

"Three fifty," I said, unable to believe how quickly time had passed in the rush of customers, and that I hadn't noticed. Lexi and I had impersonated a pair of spinning tops since opening the store this morning. It was sure to be a record-high sales day, and I'd been so thrilled I hadn't noticed a friend's four-hour delay.

I needed to hire more help.

But first I needed to make sure Louisa was okay.

"I'll call her," I said. "I'm sure she's just tied up with her research." She'd planned to stop by the property-investments office and ask Gus about the insurance company Ben used. Maybe that had led her on a bunny trail, chasing leads. I certainly knew what that was like.

A chill ran through me as I dialed, the thought of her alone with one of my suspects wasn't a pleasant one.

I scanned the street beyond my shop window as I waited for Louisa to pick up.

And the familiar white pickup truck came into view across the square.

"Well?" Sutton pressed.

"No answer." I left a voicemail then disconnected and switched gears. "I'm going to try her neighbor."

I dug the hen-shaped business card from my purse and dialed Mary while watching the truck for signs of motion inside. Had Mary really spent the day in Bliss enjoying the town or had she been here stalking me as I'd initially suspected? And why did I take everyone's statements as truth?

The call went to voicemail as well.

I chewed my lip and dragged my gaze over the crowded sidewalks in search of Mary. Was she here? Is that why she wasn't answering? Had she done something to Louisa? Was she planning to do something to me next?

I dialed her again.

"Hello?" a woman answered. Wind blew into the receiver, slightly muffling the voice.

"Mary?" I asked. "This is Bonnie Balfour. Louisa's friend

from Bliss." I locked eyes with Sutton, hoping we were both worried for nothing.

Despite what the trees allegedly said.

"Oh, hey." Mary's voice grew clear as the wind died down. She sounded bored and less than thrilled to find me on the other end of her line. "I'm feeding the hens, and I need to get them into their house for the night. Did you just call a minute ago and hang up?"

"No," I said too quickly, then cringed as I recalled a pesky advancement in technology called Caller ID. "I mean, yes. I called, but it went to voicemail." I focused on the truck outside and tried to sort the background noises coming from Mary's end of the line. Was she really at home feeding her hens?

The distinct cluck of chickens came into focus and not a single sound I'd associate with the town square. No merry chatter or gentle hum of traffic. No music drifting from nearby shops.

"You're not on the square," I said, body tensing as my mind raced.

If Mary was truly at home, who had the truck outside my shop again?

"Obviously," she said. "And I'm kind of in the middle of something, so —."

"Did you let someone borrow your truck?" I asked, pressing on and inching around the counter for a better look across the square.

"I don't have a truck," she said.

"Yes, you do," I argued. "A white pickup. It was outside your house when I stopped yesterday, and I've seen you driving it."

"Ugh," she said. "Hang on." The decibel of chicken commotion rose in the background, along with a string of thumping sounds that made me think she'd dropped the phone.

Another set of customers approached the register, and I did my best to ring them up and make change without looking upset while waiting for Mary to return.

"Okay," Mary said with a huff, as I sent the final customer away with an authentic smile. "The hens are in. Now, what were you asking me? Never mind. I remember," she said, regaining her irritation. "It's a community truck. We all use it."

"You have a community truck?"

"Well, I mean, Meadowbrook does. It saves on emissions and lowers our collective footprint. Plus it's not like most of us make enough money to afford our own vehicle, so this works."

I swallowed a large lump, now occupying my very dry throat. "Who has the pickup now?"

"I don't know. Why?" she asked, her hostile tone growing curious. "What's going on?"

I moved closer to the window, eyes fixed on the truck. "Louisa was supposed to be here hours ago, and she didn't show. Now that truck is across the square, and I'm sure I've seen it a half-dozen times since Ben Reid died. I think whoever is in it could be stalking me. And Louisa's calls are going to voicemail, so I'm afraid that same person could've done something to her."

Mary swore. "I'll go check on her. I'll call you back at this number."

"Thank y—."

The call disconnected as the pickup began to move.

I watched with breathless anticipation as it rolled around the square and passed my shop.

Eli Fogle was behind the wheel.

.   .   .

I grabbed my things and Peanut, then filled Lexi and Sutton in on the situation before making a beeline through the door.

"Peanut's got this," Sutton called, trailing after me onto the sidewalk.

I hoped she was right, because I didn't have anything other than a terrible feeling and the need to act.

I pulled into traffic several cars behind Eli and the pickup, determined to follow him and hopefully find Louisa in the process. If Mary called back to say Louisa was fine, I'd still make the trip to Meadowbrook. When I got there, I'd demand she tell me what she'd meant before about Eli. Then I could warn Louisa properly if her crush was a homicidal maniac.

Eli crossed a set of railroad tracks a moment before the arm came down, and I changed plans, taking a hard right and heading for Cromwell from a different route, avoiding the train.

I slid my cell phone into the holder on my dash and poked the screen. "Call Louisa Eggers," I told the device.

The call rang slowly as I motored away from town, winding around the less traveled roads toward Meadowbrook.

"You have reached Louisa Eggers," the voicemail began.

I disconnected with a groan and smacked my steering wheel. "Call..." I paused, unable to call Mary. I hadn't programmed her number into my contacts.

"Call Mason," I said instead, a fresh dose of adrenaline rushing through my veins.

Mason would know what to do, and he would fix this. Whatever it was. He'd told me he was close to arresting the killer, so he clearly knew more than I did. If I told him what I was doing and why, he'd know if Louisa was in danger or if I was overreacting.

I really hoped it was the latter.

"You've reached the voicemail of Sheriff Mason Wright," the recording began.

"Gah!" I scream-growled at my windshield, sending my vexation into the waning afternoon sunlight.

It was after four now, and it would be dark before six. I had an hour to find Louisa before things became significantly more dicey. So, I pressed the gas pedal harder and clung tight to the wheel as I blew past the Welcome to Cromwell sign.

I left Mason a message, blurting the situation into the air and hoping he'd play it back soon. Then I hung up and called him back repeatedly until the little dirt path into Meadowbrook appeared.

My phone rang as Mary's home came into view, and Mason's blessed face appeared on my screen.

"Thank goodness," I whispered, yanking the device to my ear. "Did you get my message?"

"I didn't listen to it," he said. "If you're calling on repeat, it's not good, and I didn't want to waste any time. Are you okay?"

"I'm fine, but I'm worried." I gave him a rundown as I slowed to examine Mary's dark home. "She went to check on Louisa," I explained, catching him up completely. "Now it doesn't look as if she's home, and she didn't answer her phone earlier."

"You're in Meadowbrook now?" Mason asked. "Stay where you are. I can be there in fifteen minutes."

"Okay, but I want to take a look at Louisa's house. Maybe Mary's there."

"Just shift into park and wait," he said. An engine growled to life on the other end of the line. "I'm at the sheriff's department in Bliss, but I'm leaving now."

I shook my head as I rolled to a stop outside Louisa's cottage. "Louisa's house is dark too."

"Bonnie," he snapped. "Stay put."

"Mason," I scolded, returning his tone. "Meet me at Louisa's." I climbed out and a dozen chickens came running. "Uh oh. She didn't put her hens away," I told him. That couldn't be good. It'd sounded as if Mary was stuffing her chickens into their house one by one when we'd talked. She'd needed to get them safely inside before she went to check on Louisa. But Louisa's hens were running wild, and the sun was setting soon.

I pulled Peanut into my arms, superstitiously hoping Sutton was right and this cactus could possibly save the day.

"What are you saying about the hens?" Mason asked.

A pair of legs came into view as I approached the backyard, the toes of brown boots pointed skyward in the green grass. "I think someone's on the ground," I said, rushing toward the feet.

Mason began to cuss valiantly as the engine sounds increased.

I skidded to a stop at the corner of Louisa's cottage.

Mary Acres was out cold on the ground. "Mary!"

Peanut's pot clunked heavily against the ground as I abandoned him in favor of getting to her side.

"Mary!" I tapped her cold cheeks with my fingers, then peeled her eyelids open when she didn't budge or complain. "She's unresponsive," I reported. "Send an ambulance." I pressed two fingers against her neck and waited for signs of life.

"Is she breathing?"

"Yeah," I said, sighing in relief. "Her pulse is thin and thready, but I found it. It's here."

Unlike Louisa, who didn't seem to be anywhere.

I scanned the shadowy land and nearby trees. "Louisa," I called, moving the phone away from my mouth to protect Mason's hearing. "Louisa!"

A distant scream ripped through the air, and I stilled. "Did you hear that?" I whispered, returning the phone to my ear.

"No," Mason said. "Bonnie, I need you to listen to me. Get back in your car."

I turned in a small circle, attempting to pinpoint the direction from which the sound had come. "I think I heard someone scream."

"Bonnie," he warned.

The scream came again, and I bolted into action, clutching my phone in hand.

"She's in the woods!" I yelled into the receiver. "Hurry!"

CHAPTER TWENTY-TWO

I ran through the forest, crunching over fallen twigs, limbs and leaves, following the sound of Louisa's voice. Soon the rush of running water broke into my consciousness, and her cries went silent. "I hear water," I told Mason, huffing as I slowed to scan the scene before me. "There's a brook that outlines the far side of the community. I saw it on a map. What if she's in the water? Do you think she can swim?" How deep could the brook be?

I hurried toward the water, keeping watch for signs of a murderous kidnapper and tuning in keenly to the forest sounds. I wished desperately for the ability to track her somehow. But Louisa wasn't Hansel or Gretel, and my panicked brain wasn't in any condition to identify a trail of bread crumbs, let alone follow them.

"I'm sending Cromwell PD," Mason said. "Go back to Louisa's cottage and wait with Mary."

"Not a chance," I said sharply, angry with whoever was behind all this, and taking out my frustrations on Mason without caring. "Mary's out cold. No one is hurting her. Louisa is screaming. She's the one in immediate danger."

"And you're going to do what?" he challenged. "Besides scare me half to death and get yourself hurt. Or worse."

"I'm going to bring her back," I said, wondering how far behind me Eli might be. I'd taken a short cut, but he hadn't been stopped by the train.

The brook came into view, and I spotted an old shed. Stacks of firewood stood in tidy rows outside. Piles of chunked trees lay beside a massive stump, an ax lodged into the top.

"There's a building," I whispered, inching closer.

Hadn't Eli been chopping wood the day he was released from Cromwell PD?

"Bonnie," Mason growled.

I crept to the side of what appeared to be an old fishing shack or maybe a woodcutter's home, then lifted onto my toes for a look through the window.

Louisa sat inside, struggling against a rope that bound her wrists behind her back. Her ivory skin was pink and puffy from stress and tears. The normally perfect barrel curls around her shoulders were a frizzy, fuzzy wreck. Thelma's pink bedazzled carrier sat at her feet.

"I see her," I said. "And I think she has Thelma." My heart swelled for their reunion, and for my good luck. Louisa was the only human in sight.

I moved to the door and checked over both shoulders before slipping carefully inside. "I've got them," I told Mason, smiling when her eyes met mine.

"Thank goodness," she croaked, throat likely raw from screaming. "Help me with the binds."

"We'll meet you at Louisa's cottage," I said, hurrying behind her to set her free. "If you see Eli, stop him." I tucked the phone into my coat pocket without disconnecting.

"I can't believe you're here," Louisa said, wiggling more frantically. "How is this possible?"

I dug my frozen fingers into the knots, and the hen inside the carrier screamed.

Bawk-aw!

"Are you okay?"

"Yeah," Louisa said. "I found Thelma in this cabin after I met with the insurance lady and the local vet. Ben had her implanted with a tracking chip! Can you believe that? I got the app for my phone and followed her beacon to this place. I made it all the way home before things went south." She wiggled her hands to help me loosen the binds, which were apparently tied by a professional knot maker.

I thought again of the brooding outdoorsman Louisa liked so much. "We have to hurry. Eli has to be in Meadowbrook by now," I said, wondering again if he'd come to Bliss in search of me. Had he intended to drag me back here as well? To what end?

I shoved the thought immediately away, not liking the myriad answers popping into mind.

"Eli's coming?" she croaked. "Thank goodness."

I paused. "What?"

"Eli's excellent with knots," she said. "He can get these loose if you can't. He's the one who taught Mrs. Pankin." She growled low in her throat and began to tug and thrash her wrists again.

"Mrs. Pankin?"

"She's lost her ever-loving mind," Louisa said.

"Why would she do this?" I asked, working diligently on the knots.

"I have no idea. She was at my place when I got back with Thelma, and I was so excited, I started telling her everything. About the way I'd called Gus and got the name of the insurance agent Ben used for personal situations. About taking that lady a soufflé. How I pretended to be from Ben's office, following up on a prized hen. She pointed me to the

Cromwell livestock vet, who'd implanted my baby with a tracking device." Louisa craned her neck to look back at me as I worked the ropes at her wrists. "Can you believe that? I swear I hate to speak ill of the dead, but he was just pure awful. I was such a complete moron to date him."

"Where's Mrs. Pankin now?" I asked, cracking a fingernail and bending another backward until it bled.

"I don't know. She left as soon as she tied me up. She probably ran off to save her sorry hide."

"Historically, I'm not that lucky," I said. In fact, given my history, Mrs. Pankin was likely lurking nearby, waiting for an opportunity to ambush us.

"Good thing I have excellent luck," Louisa said. "I found my hen and my new friend is currently rescuing me. That's a pretty good day if you don't mind the abduction part."

"I mind," I assured her. "But Mason's on the way along with Cromwell PD and an ambulance."

A sudden gust of wind rattled the cabin's windows, and I felt the brewing of a panic attack. "Tell me more about how you got here," I prompted, nudging my torn fingernails between twists of itchy rope and begging my mind to stay in control.

"I was telling Mrs. Pankin about how crazy this all was, the tracking chip and Thelma being at a cabin in Meadowbrook this whole time. Then I remembered looking at the map of this place at the Chamber of Commerce, and how the records department didn't show Ben or his company owning any substantial amount of land out here. So, I asked her who owned this property, and she said she didn't know. Then I said we could find out with a quick search on the auditor's site. I was searching it on my phone when Mrs. Pankin grabbed Thelma's carrier and pointed a tiny gun at me!"

I gave the ropes a final wiggle, and they unraveled enough for Louisa to slip free.

She stood with a sigh of relief. "Thanks!"

"Let's go," I said. The sooner we met up with Mason, the sooner this nightmare would end.

We peeked outside before hurrying into the fading day.

"Mrs. Pankin brought me back here and made me be still while she tied me up," Louisa said, clutching the hen's carrier to her chest as she ran. "She said I had to comply or she'd hurt Thelma. I did what she said, figuring someone would come for me eventually. People are always at my door. I thought for sure they'd wonder where I'd gone and start looking. I've been screaming my head off for hours."

I lifted a finger to my lips, encouraging her to keep her voice down as we made our ways back. "Mrs. Pankin hasn't left Meadowbook," I whispered. "When I realized you'd missed our lunch plans and weren't answering your phone, I called Mary."

Louisa wrinkled her nose. "Why her?"

"I didn't have anyone else's number here. She went to check on you right away. I didn't even have to ask."

Louisa slowed, and her expression went soft. "I knew she was nice. I don't know why she tries so hard to hide it."

"Well it didn't do her a lot of good this time. She's been knocked out cold in your yard," I said. "I'm guessing she ran into Mrs. Pankin."

"At least she didn't shoot her."

I frowned at Louisa's back as she took the lead again. "You really do look for a silver lining. Don't you?"

"I try," she said.

Thelma clucked wildly inside her carrier, then gave a mighty *bawk-aw!*

And Mrs. Pankin stepped into view several feet away, a small gun raised in our direction.

Louisa stopped short.

I scanned the path ahead of us, where the pale yellow of Louisa's cabin was visible through the trees.

Mrs. Pankin fixed hot eyes on me. "I knew you were behind this," she grouched. "Louisa never caused any trouble before you came along."

"I haven't killed anyone," I said. "You abducted your friend and knocked out your neighbor. You stole a chicken." I was hardly the one causing trouble here.

She narrowed her beady black eyes, gray hair fluttering in the minute breeze. "I'm trying to save our home," she said. "What was I supposed to do? First a property-investments group wanted to buy this place and turn it into a commercialized spa vacation, and now you want to villainize me for putting a stop to it?"

Louisa released Thelma's crate with one hand, holding tight with the other. She stretched the free arm in front of me, creating a barrier between me and the gun-wielding nut. "He never bought any of our land," she said. "The farmcation wasn't going to happen." Her voice cracked, and I knew she was processing the bigger truth. Mrs. Pankin hadn't only stolen her chipped chicken, she'd killed her ex-boyfriend. She wasn't just angry or lashing out in desperation, doing things that could be taken back. She was a killer, and she had no remorse.

"He was buying out our families," Mrs. Pankin seethed. "Did you think the Flickers and the Whites moved on their own? Left their donkeys and suddenly uprooted a life they'd spent so long settling into?"

"Ben bought their properties?" Louisa asked, disbelief evident in her words.

I groaned inwardly. "You didn't see any record of the property-investments company owning portions of land large enough to have a farmcation, but you sorted the results by size," I whispered. "Ben had purchased small individual plots." Apparently with plans to slowly buy them all.

"He tried to buy my land," Mrs. Pankin said, voice shaking to match Louisa's. "I hold the second-largest piece of this pie, so he came for me first. When I refused every offer he presented, he started talking to individual families. And they started saying yes."

"Aw," Louisa said softly. "I had no idea. I'm so sorry."

Mrs. Pankin wiped a falling tear away with the hand holding her gun, and I wished I'd have known the move was coming so we could've take the opportunity to run. "My family and the other Meadowbrookers gave up everything for this place," she said. "Everything! I'm the last of the original settlers, and I still give everything to keep our community going. To make it feel like one family. To help us all thrive."

Louisa tensed. "You tell us to be kind and show compassion. How could you do this? No matter your intentions."

Mrs. Pankin's head turned as the blessed sound of sirens finally echoed in the distance.

"Here they come!" Louisa shouted, pointing over the older woman's shoulder.

Mrs. Pankin spun away, gun raised to defend against no one.

Louisa grabbed my wrist, and we ran. She was lithe and surefooted, despite the long dress and pet crate in hand.

Thelma clucked wildly.

I willed myself not to look back as we made a wide arc away from the gunwoman, then back toward the sirens.

Mrs. Pankin hollered behind us, demanding we stop.

A gunshot cracked through the fading light as emergency flashers illuminated the sky overhead.

We screamed in unison, then burst onto the lawn and past Mary to the road.

A shriek erupted behind us, and Mrs. Pankin's gun fired again.

Louisa and I dropped to the ground.

My body curved over hers, as she curled around Thelma's crate.

First responders leapt from ambulances and squad cars, parked only a few yards away.

Mason's white Jeep careened into view, turfing lawns and cutting around the larger vehicles before rocking to a stop only a stone's throw away.

Eli climbed from the white pickup truck parked across the lane and followed on Mason's heels as he ran.

I dared a look in the direction of Mrs. Pankin's sudden silence and found her face down beside Mary, arms splayed and gun missing. Peanut's planter was overturned at her feet.

"That was anticlimactic," I said.

Louisa rose to join me in staring at the older, immobile woman. "Did she trip?"

Mason pulled me into a hug that erased everything else from my world.

I wrapped my arms around him and soaked in the perfection.

Paramedics bolted past us to the prone ladies.

"She fell down," Louisa said.

Eli grunted. "I heard a gunshot as I was getting home," he said. "I saw the emergency crew behind me and thought something had happened to you. I stopped at your place, then they stopped with me."

I rolled my head against Mason's chest, peering up at Louisa's lumberjack. "You were right to worry. She was abducted."

"Abducted!" Eli turned to Louisa, eyes tight and filled with fury.

Mason gathered me tighter in his arms and moved us away from the others. "Are you okay?" he asked, pressing kisses to my hair, my temple, my crown. "I don't think I've ever been that afraid in my life. It was awful. You can't imagine."

"I'm okay," I said. "Thanks for coming."

He groaned a laugh, then rested his chin on my head.

We watched in momentary silence as the paramedics worked on Mary and Mrs. Pankin.

"Sutton sent that plant with me to save Louisa," I told him. "I abandoned it when I heard her scream, and Mrs. Pankin tripped over it while chasing us. She must've knocked herself out when she fell. I think she's the one who hurt Mary before I got here."

Mary moaned as EMTs moved her onto a backboard. "Louisa," she said.

"I'm here," Louisa answered, moving quickly in her direction. "I'm okay. Thank you for coming here to check on me."

Mary made another pained sound. "Don't mention it. Ever."

"Do Sutton's plants do anything else?" Mason asked. "Or just attack people?"

I laughed and buried my face against his chest once more. "I'll have to ask."

A Cromwell police officer dropped the fallen handgun into an evidence bag.

Louisa patted Mary's hand as she was wheeled away on a gurney. She turned to Mason and me with a wrinkled brow. "It seems we've got a lot of information to sort, and Thelma needs to be fed. Can I interest you in tea?"

Eli took the carrier from Louisa and followed her onto the cottage porch.

Mason lifted a hand. "Give us a minute." He pulled back an inch after Louisa and Eli entered the cottage. "I was really scared today. More than before. Differently than before."

"I'm sorry I worried you," I said. "I never mean to upset you."

"I know. I think it was worse for me this time because I'm completely, hopelessly in love with you," he said softly, caressing my frozen cheek and pressing a kiss to my lips.

Tears bloomed in my eyes. "You love me?"

He smiled. "I know we're supposed to be taking things slowly, and believe me, I've told myself that repeatedly, but my love for you is like an instinct. It's bone-deep and unwavering. I love you like it's my purpose in this life and in this world. And if it paid the bills, I'd gladly quit my day job to do only that."

I smiled as the tears fell, and I kissed him again, enjoying how completely this day had turned around. "I love you too."

CHAPTER TWENTY-THREE

"Happy Valentine's Day," I told Gigi, wrapping her in a tight embrace and kissing her cheek loudly. "You did it!"

Opening day at Oh My Goodies had been a tremendous success, and I was honored to be part of the memories.

Mason and I had arrived early in the morning, offering her four extra hands. She'd readily accepted and had needed us both from open to close. Now, the shelves were bare, the inventory sold, and the after-party was ready to begin.

Dad swapped the soft instrumental music playing through hidden speakers for some lively jazz we all knew was Gigi's favorite.

She grinned. "Yes, we did," she said, eyes bright.

Mama flipped the hand painted OPEN/CLOSED sign on the bakery front door and shouted, "That's a wrap!"

The little crowd of Gigi's family and close friends raised their hands and voices in cheers.

The bakery had been busy from sun up to sun down, and that was worth a celebration. Everyone took turns congratulating Gigi, hugging her and complimenting her beautiful new shop.

Mirabelle and Sutton hauled trays of special cakes, cookies and chocolate-covered whatnots onto the counter for partygoers to sample and enjoy.

Mama and Dad moved in to gush over Gigi, and I took a step back to admire the view.

Soft scents of warm vanilla, caramel and spun sugar seemed to cling to the walls and hang in the air. Strands of paper hearts hung in swoops from the ceiling. It was possibly my favorite Valentine's Day ever.

Times like these made it impossible to imagine why I'd ever wanted to leave this place or these people. It was a mistake I'd never make again.

"Gigi?" Mason called, turning me and several others in his direction. "I've got it all packed up. Is there anything else I can do?"

I dragged my gaze over the length of him while Gigi considered her answer.

He'd dressed up for the occasion, opting for a white long-sleeved shirt and black dress pants instead of his usual t-shirt and jeans. He'd shaved and gotten a haircut too, which I thought was sweet. Though my favorite look on him these days was uber casual. Socked feet on my kitchen floor. Mussy hair and scruffy cheeks after a long nap curled with Clyde and me on the couch.

It was a look I'd had the privilege of seeing several times since he'd first told me he loved me outside Louisa's cottage. It was a look I hoped to see many more times to come.

"What?" he asked, moving in my direction, when he caught me staring.

I'd completely missed Gigi's response to his question.

"I'm just looking at you," I said.

He pumped his brows, and I laughed.

Logically, it made no sense for me to love again so soon after an ugly divorce. It defied all sense of self-preservation. I'd had the argument with myself a thousand times, and it always ended the same way. If I wouldn't guard my own heart, then who would guard it for me?

The answer was always the same.

Mason.

Mason would selflessly and doggedly guard my heart at all costs, for as long as I asked him. And I trusted him completely with the job.

So, no, loving him wasn't logical, and maybe someday I'd learn it also wasn't smart, but for now, it felt brave, hopeful and a little defiant to dare such a wild thing. To take a second chance at love.

He looped long arms around my back and smiled down at me. "Looking at me, huh?"

"I'm always looking at you." I rose onto my toes and kissed him.

Someone cleared their throat, and we pulled apart by an inch.

Eli smiled over Louisa's shoulder. He wore a blue t-shirt under a brown barn coat with jeans and boots. She looked like the heroine on a poster for a period piece, as usual. Navy gingham dress, barrel curls pulled up at the temples with a matching bow and simple brown boots with cream tights. The only thing missing was her funny-feathered hen and best friend, Thelma.

She wiggled her fingers in a shy, hip-high wave. "We had to stop and congratulate Gigi. The place looks amazing."

"The goodies are phenomenal," Eli said, popping a square of pound cake into his mouth.

I rearranged myself to lean against Mason's side. My red silk blouse and black dress pants with flats seemed instantly modern and flashy in the other couple's presence.

Not that Eli and Louisa were a couple. *Yet.*

The men shook hands, and Louisa blushed furiously.

I could only guess why.

"I hoped to catch you before you headed out," Eli said. "I imagine Valentine's plans are in the works?"

Mason grinned. "I imagine you're right."

I looked to Louisa, wondering if she and Eli had some plans as well, but she glanced away, cheeks scorching pink once more.

"I heard through the grapevine Mrs. Pankin is staying in jail for a while," Eli said. "I wondered if you can say anything about that. She was a really nice lady, until she wasn't. It's shaken the community more than you'd think."

I offered a small smile, understanding from his tone that he was one of those folks struggling with what the Meadowbrook matriarch had done.

Mason shifted, pulling me close, as he always did when this subject came up. "She was moved to the state prison for safe keeping. She'll be there for the foreseeable future, and she's undergoing some psychiatric evaluations. How's Mary doing?"

"Better," Louisa said. "I've been helping her with her hens while she recovers from the concussion."

"That sounds fun," I teased, recalling the way Mary had complained extensively about Louisa. Being cared for by her perceived nemesis must feel like insult upon injury. Which I assumed would only make Mary crankier.

"She's really not so bad once you get to know her," Louisa said. "She can be a little snippy, but I'm sure that's just her protective shell talking."

I smiled, refreshed by her eternal optimism. "How are you and Thelma?"

"Excellent," she said. "I had the awful tracker removed. The whole thing has been terribly traumatic for her, but I made her a roost in my cottage and another in the soufflé shop, so she can be with me while I get things together."

"Very nice," I said. "I'm sure she appreciates it."

"Thank you. I think she does. I hope to open the shop as soon as my egg supply is replenished. Polish hens aren't great layers, but I could use your help with the décor in the meanwhile."

"Call anytime," I said.

Eli tipped his head and stepped closer to Mason, a serious expression still in place. "Can I ask you something?"

Mason dipped his chin.

"I've been trying to get my head around how Pankin managed to get the jump on Ben. He was half her age and had at least fifty pounds on her. Was he a terrible swimmer, or is she a lot stronger than she looks?"

Mason shifted, frown deepening. "According to her official statement, she lured him to the lake under guise of a meeting to discuss the sale of her land. She hid until he arrived, then snuck up behind him and hit him with a shovel."

"Oh my goodness," Louisa gasped.

I grimaced, having heard the story before. It didn't get any easier the second time.

"The impact knocked him out and into the water, where he drowned, which was her plan, so premeditation will add a lot of years to her sentence."

"Wow," Eli said softly, running an anxious hand through his thick dark hair.

"Yeah," Mason agreed. "Nothing but bats in that bonnet."

Louisa seemed to deflate with the story. "I know she wanted to protect our community, but I hate that she chose violence as her answer."

The men grunted in quiet agreement.

"Wait," I said, recalling Louisa tied to a chair with Thelma at her feet. "Why did she take your chicken?"

Louisa raised and lowered her shoulders in a slow, dramatic shrug, then looked to Mason for answers.

I turned to him as well.

"Also part of her big plan," he said, dragging a comically bland expression in my direction. "She thought she could make it look as if Ben stole the hen, then left town. She had no idea the hen was implanted with a tracking device and sincerely thought Ben would sink. Apparently a childhood friend of hers drowned in a cold lake when she was young, and locals dragged the bottom to find her. Cooler temperatures typically decrease the odds of bodies rising." He rubbed his forehead as we all cringed. "Here's an irrelevant twist," he said. "I had an off-the-record chat with the attorney Ben used to draw up that paperwork for a partial-custody suit. Apparently, it had nothing to do with his belief Thelma could be an animal actor or star in commercials. He didn't even think he could win. He just wanted to keep Louisa in court as long as it took to drain her trust."

I looked to Louisa. She'd said her family was a staple in Cromwell, and I'd assumed that meant they had money, but there hadn't been a mention of any trust.

She covered her mouth, brows pinched in anger. "Why would he do that?"

Mason glanced quickly to me, then Eli, before returning his attention to Louisa. "He knew you owned nearly as much of Meadowbrook as Mrs. Pankin, that you have a troubled relationship with your family, and that you'd spend every penny you had to save your hen. With your bank account depleted and no way to secure additional funds or financially manage your extensive acreage, you'd be forced to sell to him, and he'd push ahead with the farmcation with or without Mrs. Pankin's land."

Her jaw dropped and her hand fell to her side. "Monster."

"What turned you on to Pankin?" Eli asked, daring a sideways look at Louisa.

Did he want to reach out and comfort her? Was he surprised to learn she owned such a large piece of their community's land?

I was.

"She seemed so wholesome and maternal to me," Eli continued, speaking of Mrs. Pankin. "I never would've believed it if anyone other than Louisa had seen that side of her firsthand."

Mason nodded. "She reached her breaking point when she thought the investment company was going to ruin what she'd spent her life building, and she snapped. Fortunately, she's not a criminal mastermind, and it didn't take long for us to find a series of calls between her and Ben, then to realize she was the last person he'd likely spoken with before he died. From there, the case practically built itself."

Eli slid his eyes in Louisa's direction, then flipped his attention to me. "It's almost as if these two didn't have to get involved at all or be threatened at gun point."

I pointed at Eli, and Louisa's blush returned.

She raised a finger in question. "So, Mrs. Pankin was probably spending so much time with me, volunteering to help with Jack and Jill, making me tea and chatting about my soufflé stand, because she wanted to collect information on Ben and the farmcation?"

Mason offered a sad smile. "I'm sure she just enjoyed your company. I hear everyone does."

Louisa looked away a moment before her eyes flicked to mine.. "She was with me when I remembered I had a key to Ben's place, and I told her I was considering a look inside."

Mason's usual frown returned, and his tight gaze turned to me.

"Ugh," Louisa continued. "She was keeping tabs on me the whole time. I thought she was keeping me company because Thelma was gone."

Eli rocked back on his heels. "Sticking by you was a smart move. Everyone visits your place. Who knows how much community gossip is spoken there on a daily basis." He looked to Mason with an odd mix of awe and annoyance. "Her cottage practically needs a revolving door."

Gigi appeared at Louisa's side, hauling Sutton and Gretchen behind her. "I have folks for you to meet," she said.

Louisa turned toward them with a broad smile, and Eli moved with her, like a magnet.

Mason tugged me back a few steps, then spun me to face him. "Before I forget," he said. "I want to tell you how proud I am of you for the way you handled your ex. Also, I made a couple calls and learned your letter to his attorney helped him avoid jail time, as promised."

"Yay," I said flatly, unsure why Mason would bring Grant up on Valentine's Day.

"You'll be entertained to know he was assigned community service instead."

My cheeks lifted in a cautious smiled. "Tell me more."

"As a replacement for jail time, your high-class ex will soon be sporting a state-issued orange jumpsuit and collecting trash from local parks and highways, straight through the unrelenting heat of summer."

"I'm ashamed at how happy that makes me."

Mason laughed. "I thought that might make you smile, and you were looking pretty bummed about Mrs. Pankin."

I nodded, still smiling. "Picking up trash in public is so much worse than being hidden away in a white-collar prison," I whispered.

"Well, he did ask, repeatedly, for a letter to help him avoid jail. You only did what he wanted," Mason said. "And I haven't said this before, but I'm also proud of you for seeing your counselor regularly and working through the tough stuff. I know how hard that can be, and how scary. You make it look easy."

I hooked my arm with his and leaned into him. "You're proud of me."

"Very."

Because I was his to be proud of, I thought, *his friend, his significant other, his confidant.* The truth of it made me infinitely more elated and less afraid.

"Thank you," I said. "Though I still wish you'd talk to me about whatever has been on your mind."

He smiled. "How about we let tonight be about Gigi, and I promise to talk to you about my thing as soon as I'm ready? I'll tell you, and only you, as soon as I can, but it's nothing for you to worry about. I promise."

I weighed his words and smiled again, thrilled to be so trusted and eager to know what he was struggling with so I could help. "Deal."

Cami and Dale made their way along the narrow hallway from the back door, bringing a gust of chilly wind with them. The goofy looks on their faces suggested they'd enjoyed their time outside very much.

Dale lifted his chin at Mason when the couple approached. "Got a minute?"

"Yep." Mason pressed a kiss to my temple, then followed Dale back down the hallway and outside.

Cami turned to me, perfect brows furrowing.

"What was that about?" I asked, staring into the empty hall.

"I don't know," she said. "He checked his phone on our way back inside because it'd buzzed a few times while we were out there. He held the door for me and said he wanted to see Mason before we headed home. I didn't expect them to walk away like that."

I chewed my lip, curiosity fully piqued. "Any idea who called?"

Cami slid her eyes my way. "No, but he's been acting squirrely for a while, and I don't like it."

"That's what I said about Mason."

Her dark eyes narrowed. "What are we going to do about it?" "I don't know. Mason told me he'd let me know what was going on with him as soon as he was ready." I gnawed on my lip, trying to stick to my promise and let him tell me in his time.

Cami pulled her phone from her back pocket and scrolled to a familiar name. "I don't like it, and I know how we can find out what those two are up to without an extended wait." Then she hit Send on a call to Special Agent Cat Rawlings.

THANK YOU SO MUCH FOR READING EYELET WITNESS! I HOPE YOU'LL ENJOY EACH NEW STORY IN THE BONNIE & CLYDE MYSTERIES MORE THAN THE LAST AND THAT YOU'LL KEEP IN TOUCH BETWEEN THE BOOKS!

I ALSO HOPE YOU'LL TAKE A MOMENT TO LEAVE A REVIEW IF YOU ENJOYED THIS STORY. REVIEWS ARE AUTHOR-GOLD AND SO APPRECIATED!

And if you're ready for the next Bonnie & Clyde adventure, you can order FLARED STIFF now!

-AND-

Join Thelma & Louisa in Meadowbrook for NO FARM NO FOWL, their series debut!

ABOUT THE AUTHOR

Julie Anne Lindsey is an award-winning and bestselling author of mystery and romantic suspense. She's published more than forty novels since her debut in 2013 and currently writes series as herself, as well as under the pen names **Bree Baker**, **Jacqueline Frost**, and **Julie Chase**.

When Julie's not creating new worlds or fostering the epic love of fictional characters, she can be found in Kent, Ohio, enjoying her blessed Midwestern life. And probably plotting murder with her shamelessly enabling friends. Today she hopes to make someone smile. One day she plans to change the world.